White Snake
and Other Stories

by Geling Yan

Translated by Lawrence A. Walker

白
蛇

Aunt Lute Books

San Francisco

Copyright ©1999 by Geling Yan

First Edition
10 9 8 7 6 5 4 3 2 1

Aunt Lute Books
P.O. Box 410687
San Francisco, CA 94141

Senior Editor: Joan Pinkvoss
Managing Editor: Shay Brawn

Cover photo: Chase Chen, courtesy of Stratosphere Entertainment
Cover and text design: Kajun Design
Typesetting: Kajun Design

Production: Corey Cohen, Gina Gemello, Shahara Godfrey, Golda Sargento, Livia Tenzer, Pimpila Thanaporn

This book was funded in part by a grant from the National Endowment for the Arts.

ISBN: 1-879960-55-9

Library of Congress Cataloging-in-Publication Data

Yen , Ko-ling.
White snake and other stories / by Geling Yan ; translated by Lawrence A. Walker.
p.   cm.
Contents: White snake — Celestial bath — The death of the lieutenant — Red apples — Nothing more than male and female — Siao yu.
ISBN 1-879960-55-9
1. Yen, Ko-ling Translations into English.   I. Walker, Lawrence A., 1956-   . II. Title.
PL2925.K55A28 1999
895.1'352–dc21   99-23507
                                                                    CIP

Translator's Note

Those familiar with the author's work in Chinese may notice minor disparities between this translation and the original. In many places, as is common in Chinese prose style, the author is not specific about time, space and motion, leaving the details to the reader's imagination. It became obvious during the editing process that this indirection was sometimes confusing and distracting to Western readers. After discussion with the author, I have been able to fill in a number of these details in a manner true to her original intent.

Throughout this text, Chinese names are given with family name first and given name second, except in the case of the author.

Acknowledgments

The author would like to thank Professors John Schultz, Betty Shifflett and Constantine Tung, as well as the staff of Columbia College, Chicago for the help and encouragement they have given her over the years. She also wishes to thank Joan Chen, her old and dear friend, for turning the story "Celestial Bath" into a beautiful film.

The translator wishes to honor the memory of his grandfather, Charles Arthur Barlow, and of his former teachers and mentors, Dr. Ludwig Krabbe and Dr. Walter Samuel Getz Kohn.

Both author and translator would like to thank the staff of Aunt Lute Books, in particular Joan Pinkvoss and Shay Brawn, for turning this book from dream to reality.

The author dedicates this work to her mother, the late Jia Ling, to her father, Xiao Ma (Yan Dunxun), and to her husband, Larry Walker.

The translator dedicates his work to his mother, Dr. Billie (Lee) Barlow Walker, to his father, Dr. Lawrence David Walker, and to his wife, Geling Yan.

Contents

白蛇 White Snake

TRANSLATOR'S PROLOGUE: *This story is set mostly in the "ten years of chaos" of China's Great Proletarian Cultural Revolution (1966–76), when the social order turned upside down and traditional arts were brutally suppressed in favor of "revolutionary" models.*

Essential to understanding this story is a basic knowledge of the legend of White Snake, which is the basis of a Chinese opera. In this novella, the main character, Sun Likun, develops the White Snake story into her signature ballet.

The legend of White Snake concerns two nagas, or mythical serpents, White Snake (a female) and Blue Snake (a male), who had attained the status of Immortals and lived in the heavens. Blue Snake fell in love with White Snake and asked her to marry him. White Snake made Blue Snake a wager: they would fight a battle, and if Blue Snake won, White Snake would become his consort, but if White Snake won, then Blue Snake would turn into a female and become White Snake's maidservant. Deeply enamored of White Snake and desiring to be with her at all costs, Blue Snake accepted the challenge. White Snake won the battle, and Blue Snake became her handmaiden.

One day the pair descended to earth. They took human form as two beautiful young women, Lady White and Lady Blue, and set up residence in Hangzhou. While taking a ferry at Broken Bridge, White Snake met and fell in love with a young scholar named Xu Xian (pronounced "shyü"). They married and started a medicine shop in a town along the Yangtze River, and White Snake used her magical powers to render Xu Xian's medicines especially effective, affording them a prosperous life.

A Buddhist abbot named Fa Hai saw through her disguise and warned Xu Xian that his wife was actually a snake. He gave Xu Xian a potion to give his wife to drink which would return her to her original serpent form. Xu Xian gave her this potion and, when he gazed on her original form, promptly died of fright. White Snake then went through a great odyssey to obtain the potent lingzhi fungus to restore her husband to life.

The revived Xu Xian remained fearful of his wife and fled to the abbot's monastery for refuge. White Snake came to plead with the abbot, but to no avail. In anger, she attacked the monastery with a great horde of underwater creatures.

The battle was a draw, and the abbot came to realize that he had failed to best her because White Snake was pregnant. He advised Xu Xian to return and live with her until the child was born. Upon his return, Blue Snake almost killed Xu Xian with her sword, but White Snake intervened.

The child was born, and Fa Hai conspired with Xu Xian to have White Snake resume her original form and be imprisoned under Thunder Peak Pagoda at West Lake in Hangzhou. They succeeded in this plan, but later Blue Snake came and destroyed the pagoda and rescued White Snake. The two departed the world of mortals and re-ascended into the heavens. (This synopsis is adapted from Peking Opera and Mei Lanfang, New World Press, Beijing, 1980.)

THE OFFICIAL ACCOUNT, Part 1
A Letter to Premier Zhou Enlai

Respected and beloved Premier!

First, please allow us to express our collective wishes for long life without end for our Great Leader Chairman Mao!

All of Sichuan Province's eighty million people were deeply moved

that our Premier, in the midst of so many important and pressing matters, recently found the time to request that his personal secretary call
and inquire about the state of health of the formerly famous dancer
Sun Likun. This very clearly shows that our Premier, occupied as he is
with myriad affairs of state and heavily burdened day and night with
the work of the Revolution and the construction of our Socialist
Motherland, still constantly takes to heart the sufferings of the people. Though our province's propaganda, culture and education authorities were not directly involved in the case of Sun Likun, subsequent to
receiving your personal secretary's telephone call, and acting in accordance with the Premier's intention to protect our country's important
talents, we sent a special emissary to the provincial Performing Arts
Troupe to investigate Sun Likun's incarceration, interrogation and sen-
tencing up to the time when she suffered a mental breakdown. The
results of this investigation are as follows:

Sun Likun, female, presently 34 years of age, was formerly a major
performer in the Sichuan Province Performing Arts Troupe. In 1958 and
1959, she traveled to the Soviet Union's International Song and Dance
Festival, where she won the Stalin Prize for the Arts. In 1962 she
received First Prize in the Solo Ballet Performance category in the All-
China National Dance Competition. In 1963, Beijing Film Studios made
a film based on *The Legend of White Snake,* a ballet she both choreographed and performed in. At the same time, the stage version of the
ballet played in seventeen cities, causing quite a sensation. In order
to study and imitate the behavior of snakes, Sun had apprenticed herself to an Indian snake charmer and had helped him raise snakes. The
"snake step," which she developed on her own, became her signature
movement, and its performance received tremendous acclaim among
ballet critics. The step even became a fad among members of the
audience.

In 1966, Sun Likun was denounced by the Revolutionary Masses.
In 1969, on the basis of various investigations and Sun's own four-
hundred-plus-page self-criticism, Sun was classified as a decadent
bourgeois element, a suspected Soviet-trained spy, a seductress and a
counter-revolutionary snake-in-the-grass. She was officially placed

under investigative detention. Because Sun's place of detention was
the scenery warehouse of the provincial Performing Arts Troupe in
Chengdu, her living conditions were not overly harsh.

From 1969 onward, Sun's case was reexamined many times, but at
no point did the Revolutionary Vigilance Committee exhibit any vio-
lence toward her. As for depriving Sun of her personal freedoms, this
measure was taken by acclamation of the Revolutionary Masses subsequent to our country's self-defensive counterattack at the Sino-Soviet
border. As is the nature of a mass political movement, matters went
beyond the control of the leadership, resulting at times in extreme sit-
uations.

According to revelations of people close to the Sun Likun case,
Sun's mental illness began in December of 1971. In the period prior to
this, her guards often saw a young man in his twenties enter Sun
Likun's detention room. He carried a letter of introduction from the
Exceptional Cases Group of the Central Propaganda Ministry and
referred to himself as a special envoy from the Central Government
with the assignment of investigating Sun's case. This young man, who
wore a woolen military uniform, displayed an aggressive bullying
demeanor and gave the overall impression of being well connected.
For the duration of one month, this person entered Sun Likun's cell
every day promptly at 3:00 PM and left just as punctually at 5:00 PM
According to the statements of the guard staff, Sun showed no trace
of abnormality during this period. The young man was calm, polite and
correct in his behavior, and her morale actually showed improvement.
In fact, she was even heard practicing dance exercises late at night in
the dark.

It is reported that on a particular day the young man appeared
driving a motorcycle with a side car and demanded to take Sun Likun
to a certain provincial government guesthouse to proceed further with
their discussions. He refused to reveal the purpose of these discussions, intimating that even the highest levels of the provincial leadership did not have the authority to inquire into his handling of this
case. Because of the apparently indisputable authority of his letter of
introduction and his identifying documents, the Revolutionary

Committee agreed to release Sun Likun to his custody, for a period not to exceed six hours. At 10:00 PM sharp, the young man returned Sun Likun to her place of detention. A few days later, Sun Likun suddenly began showing signs of mental illness, talking to herself and alternately crying and laughing.

The young man disappeared from the scene. On the eve of Chinese New Year, Sun was transferred to the Psychiatric Division of the People's Hospital of Sichuan Province. The following week, Sun was moved to Joyous Song Mountain Hospital in Chongqing, our province's most highly respected research institution for mental illness. Sun responded to treatment and gradually stabilized. According to our investigation of hospital personnel, a young man came once and asked to see Sun Likun, but Sun refused to see him. We are currently conducting a systematic investigation to determine whether this was the same young man who had been reviewing her case and further to determine what caused Sun Likun's illness.

We will soon submit a report to the Premier on Sun Likun's state of health. Until then, we respectfully wish to reassure the Premier that there is no cause for concern.

In conclusion, on behalf of the eighty million people of Sichuan Province, we extend to our beloved and respected Premier our most worshipful revolutionary salute! We hope that our Premier will take the utmost care of himself for the sake of all the people of our country and the great undertaking of establishing Communism. For the sake of China's Revolution and the world's, please take care!

(signed)
Sichuan Province Revolutionary Committee
Propaganda, Culture and Education Department
March 31, 1972

(DOCUMENT CLASSIFIED FOR INTERNAL USE ONLY — DOCUMENT CONTROL NO. 00710016)

THE POPULAR ACCOUNT, Part 1

Actually, that formerly famous Sun Likun is a major international slut. Once she had a Russian-language translator help her write a letter to her Soviet paramour telling him that "the flower of our love will forever be in bloom and never wither." Though he and she were "at opposite edges of the sky," she continued, they were "yet closer than neighbors." Later, that same translator copied her letters onto big-character posters and posted them next to the sidewalk of a busy street.

During the years she was performing *The Legend of White Snake*, Sun Likun toured seventeen cities, both large and small, and in every city there were men chasing after her. That water snake waist of hers got the men coiled up in her bed in no time. All the men who slept with Sun Likun said she had 120 vertebrae. She could twist any way she felt like twisting. There wasn't a straight bone in her body. She could wind back and forth at will, so the effect was as if she had no bones at all.

Actually, she only *looked* tall. She seemed to grow two inches taller every time she raised that pointy chin of hers — and she always kept it raised, even when the masses would harangue her in struggle sessions. Her beauty was in her chin and neck. As she turned her face this way and rotated it that way, her gaze fell on no one. If ten thousand people came to her struggle session, eight thousand were there for the sole purpose of seeing her snakelike neck. Of the ten thousand, nine thousand would have seen her in *The Legend of White Snake* at least three times. People in Sichuan used to say our province had three famous products: pickled mustard roots, five-grain spirits and Sun Likun.

After Sun Likun got fat, she became an ordinary woman. Less than six months of being locked up in the Performing Arts Troupe's scenery warehouse and she looked exactly like any middle-aged woman you'd see on the street: a keg-shaped waist, gourdlike breasts, and big squarish buttocks that spread out so wide you could lay out a whole meal on them. Her face was still pretty, only broader, and her eyelashes would still sweep back and forth until you felt your heart tickle, but the black and the white of her eyes were starting to lose their clarity.

The scenery warehouse of the Performing Arts Troupe was on the second floor. Down below, the building was encircled by a wall. If you stood on the wall, you were at eye level with Sun Likun's bed. Under the bed, instead of her famous brightly colored pet snake, was a brightly colored chamber pot. Beyond the wall was a messy construction site. A building had been torn down and a new one had yet to be built, so the ground was strewn with worn-out tiles and stacks of new bricks.

On the site some idle construction workers were playing a card game on an improvised table made of bricks. They were singing:

I've seen thousands of pretty girls
But you are the prettiest in the world:
Ears like scoops, persimmon-cake face,
Green bean eyes and skinny chicken legs.

Sun Likun knew they were singing to her, trying to tease her into cheerfulness. She had been locked in there for two years already, and she was only allowed to leave the room to take a shit. First, she had to ask for permission from a guard; only if she received it could she go out the door leading down the hall to the latrine. When she needed to pee, she would do it in her chamberpot, and every night, with permission, she carried this colorful pot down the hall to dump its contents. The distance from here to there was only about ten paces, but all the while the guard would follow behind her with a big club. The Vigilance Committee guards were all teenage girls, dance students at the Performing Arts Academy. In keeping with the revolutionary operas of the last few years, they all had broad shoulders, thick legs and loud voices. Boys from the Academy weren't allowed to serve on Sun Likun's Vigilance Committee; they would have ended up serving under the vigilance of Sun Likun. The teenage girl dancers had worshipped Sun Likun. Whenever they would enter her dressing room or her private exercise room, where she'd hung the picture of herself with Premier Zhou Enlai, they would do so with the awe of one entering an ancestral shrine. Because such reverence easily turns to resentment, the girls made utterly reliable club-wielding wardens for "Ancestor" Sun Likun.

The bathroom Sun Likun used had only one working squat toilet — the other squat toilets didn't flush properly. The sole functioning toilet was directly in line with the doorway, but the girl guards did not permit Sun Likun to close the door when she squatted there. She would sit facing the young guard who formed an X across the doorway, a club dangling across her stocky thigh. In the beginning of her internment, eye-to-eye in this manner, she could squat for an hour with no results. She would beg the girls to avert their eyes. Crying real tears, she would plead, "if you don't turn your eyes away, I won't be able to do anything, even if I die of misery." But the guards absolutely would not soften their hearts. You used to be so elegant, they thought, like a celestial being. You never seemed to eat the same food or breathe the same air or shit the same shit as everyone else. Now you're just one of us ordinary folks, squatting on the latrine like millions of your fellow countrymen.

By the summer of 1970, Sun Likun had finally learned how to have a bowel movement while squatting face-to-face with one of the teenage girls. She could squat comfortably on the toilet and would spit on the floor while she waited, just like all the rest of the Chinese masses. Sun Likun had become accustomed to her ignominy. She no longer felt as if she would die of shame whenever she was called a string of nasty names.

The same crew of construction workers was still down below, singing songs and playing cards. Every once in a while they would have a political study session or lackadaisically lay a few bricks. At night they would spread out a picnic on the platform of bricks, drink seventy-cents-a-bottle orange wine and heed the wine's call to arms, shouting guess-finger drinking songs with verses like, "your mama slept with eight men, eight men."

One morning they noticed that the shutters of the upper room were open. No longer would they need to climb up to the top of the wall and peer through cracks in the shutters to catch a glimpse of that beautiful fat snake-woman. Because this day—and every day after—she appeared to them of her own will, without any self-consciousness.

The damsel in the window was as white as a spring silkworm ready to spit its silk. As she stood there—this "famous product" of Sichuan—all the construction workers, young and old, seemed frightened to see her up close for the first time. Their singing stopped. Suddenly self-conscious, the bricklayers started laying bricks and the mortar mixers started mixing mortar.

Sun Likun brushed her teeth at this window every morning. The toothbrush had very few bristles left, and the rasping it made in her mouth sounded painful. By now the workers had dared to look her in the face and smile at her openly, the old men flashing yellow teeth and the young men white. While they looked at her, they would holler, "D'ya see that? Look how white her arms are, like steamed pork buns!" They still didn't dare speak to her directly. She had been up in the heavens for so many years while they had been here below that, even though they could now look upon her face, they weren't entirely sure they now shared the world of mortals with her.

Sun Likun could hear them discussing her right below the window, arguing about all sorts of rumors surrounding her, just as if she were a painting. However they spoke about her, good or ill, there was no restraining them. Their arguments grew heated. One said, "She lived together with a snake, that's what they wrote on the big-character posters. It was a big bright-colored python. The snake slept under the bed, and she slept up on top of the bed." Another one objected, "It was a *white* python! A *white* python!" They argued back and forth, "White python!" "Bright-colored python!" observing her with one eye. Yet, for a while, she gave no indication of her confirmation or denial. Finally she interrupted: "A bright-colored python. Very sweet-tempered."

The discussions ceased for a time. So *that* was the woman in the painting. After that, there was nothing to make them feel they had to keep their distance. They were no longer the slightest bit in awe of her. After all, she was just like any fat middle-aged woman you could see at the marketplace, the kind who would prattle on mindlessly while buying a penny's worth of green onion, or who would demand to check the scales when buying two ounces of meat. All the fellows, young and old alike, were very disappointed. They saw clearly how her hair, pulled up in a bun, was long unwashed, and her cheek bore an imprint from the mat that covered her straw pillow. And everybody saw clearly that she wore an ordinary light blue blouse, tight and old, which, since she had grown fat, bound up her body like a *zongzi*. On the front of her blouse was a smear of blood from a smashed mosquito. And besides all that, this beautiful snake-woman Sun Likun could *also* devour a big bowl of noodles, and if the noodles were too spicy, she could *also* open her mouth inelegantly and slurp them down with a "shee-hoo, shee-hoo!" sound, and after eating the noodles, her exquisite, naturally pure white teeth would *also* have some red chili skins or green onion slivers caught between them. She was so down-to-earth. Everybody was really disappointed.

One night, when desire and mosquitos buzzed through the air together, several of the young men climbed the surrounding wall to see how Sun Likun protected herself under her mosquito net. Suddenly, the window was pushed open from the inside with a bang. In the window frame stood Sun Likun, striking a provocative bitchy pose, hands on her hips, wearing a sweat-soaked sleeveless undershirt, which under the dusty lamplight appeared both sticky and wrinkled.

"What's so great to look at? Tell me so I can look, too!" Sun Likun laughed spitefully.

That sleeveless undershirt she had on was truly awful; it had been washed so many times that its texture seemed to have dissolved. When she moved and the streetlights caught it, the men could see how the transparent undershirt collapsed over her flesh, leaving everything, whether concave or convex, clearly distinguishable.

Some of the young fellows were practically naked themselves, except for their briefs, yet they were more embarrassed than she. Like frogs dropping into a pond, they jumped off the wall one after the other.

"What did'ja see? Huh?" She taunted them with her victory, ever more ferocious and spiteful.

"There wasn't much to see," one of the young fellows shot back mockingly, putting on the airs of a sophisticated city boy.

"Of course there's nothing to see. Anything your mother's got, I've got!" she replied.

This last remark defeated the young men completely. Hearing her counterattack in this manner, they crossed their eyes, just as when Xu Xian pulled back the bed curtains and saw Lady White in her original snake form. They had never imagined that a woman who had been like an Immortal and a dream could so easily give up her modesty and dignity after being penned up for two years.

In the dog days, Sun Likun would stand leaning against the window frame, always in that same beat-up undershirt, batting the air with a palm-leaf fan. When the construction workers chewed melon seeds, they would share some with her. When they smoked, she would beg cigarettes off them. She quickly developed an addiction and smoked more ferociously than the men. Soon no one could afford to supply her any more, so she told them to pick up their cigarette butts off the ground and just give those to her to smoke. The young fellows piled up the butts, tore the slogans off some big-character posters, wrapped the butts up in the paper and handed them over to her. They all knew that her wages had been stopped and her bank account frozen, but then, this treatment was normal for any prisoner serving a long sentence, especially one styled as an "ox-devil snake goddess."

One day, one of the young fellows came to Sun Likun wielding a bag of cigarette butts and said, "They say you can put your foot on your head. I want to see you do that."

She crossed her arms and thought for a while, then said, "What if I don't?"

"If you don't do it, no more cigarette butts. Every time we bend over to pick up a butt, that equals one kowtow. You think that comes cheap?"

Again she thought for a while. The construction workers had stopped playing cards and carousing and were craning their necks in unison toward the window, like a gaggle of geese waiting to be fed. Suddenly, Sun Likun grabbed her heel and pointed it skyward. Her white, thick stocky leg, shaped like a daikon radish yet straight as a writing brush, suddenly swung up vertically before the eyes of her audience, her two legs together forming the numeral 1, exposing her tattered pink floral panties. The construction workers found they could not recall the proper significance of those two famous legs, because now they had so many improper connotations.

The workers were still thinking of those connotations when they pleaded and demanded that she play the other leg for them. The famous dancer Sun Likun, locked in her cagelike pen, had turned into a circus monkey, playing her formerly famous pair of legs to men, young and old, whose bodies were covered with lustful sweat. Yet when displayed in succession, her two peerlessly beautiful legs, though now thick and corpulent, testified to their inexhaustible and profound meaning, their former significance. During this display, the construction workers imagined other scenes: these legs abundant with strength yet flexible as white pythons coiling around their flesh, coiling around the downy nakedness of that pink-bodied Soviet dancer. Those two legs of hers could easily coil around ten of those furry foreigners.

Sun Likun put her leg down, leaned one shoulder against the window frame, and with her eyes half-closed eyes in a sultry expression, thrust out her palm for the cigarette butts. The young fellow standing on the wall handed her the poster-paper bag and felt his hands grazed by her fingernails. He saw her pale face flush red in that instant. Either the cigarette butts or perhaps the displaying of her legs had given her a sudden ecstatic rush.

A downy ring above her upper lip was seeped with perspiration. Her eyebrows and eyelashes were thick. It was said that this beautiful snake-woman was not a pure Han Chinese, that drops of either Hui or Qiang blood had found their way into her. The worker was so close to her he could clearly see a red mole on the bottom of her eyelid. Afterward, when he told his workmates about this mole, an older worker said it was a bad omen. It meant that this woman could never be without a man, that the space between her legs could never be idle.

It was about this time that the construction workers started carrying their buckets under her window when they washed up. Their white undershorts, when soaked through, became a second skin. As they washed, they sang,

Girl, you are like tofu lees,
Eyes so pretty men knock their knees.

Sometime in October of 1970, a very different person arrived on the scene. He was in his early twenties, neither tall nor short. His face was fresh, neither dark nor light, with two swordlike eyebrows pointing at his temples. He wore an olive woolen military uniform. In the places where the insignias had hung on the collar and shoulders, the material had a deeper hue, and the texture was newer. This was proof that the woolen uniform was real, that this young man's air of superiority was warranted. He was a "cadre kid." The woolen uniform was so broad and heavy that the young man, his slim body bent slightly forward, was almost carrying it rather than wearing it. But it was precisely the large size of his uniform and the small size of his body that gave him a peculiar air of casual elegance. The young man's strides were long, and he walked with his hands behind his back as if he were some kind of old warlord with "people clearing the way in front and a young guard running up behind."

He stood reverently on that dilapidated construction site, as if surveying an ancient battlefield. All the construction workers stopped to watch the young man, their taunting bawdy songs broken off in their mouths and the paper strips from big-character posters stuck to their hands. There was something anachronistic and unusual about this young man's appearance and bearing. The derision and disdain in his eyes made the men think he had clout. His eyes were clear and feminine; his shyness was in the dark part of his eyes, and his cruelty was in the whites. When he looked at Sun Likun, he used the dark part, and when he looked at the construction workers, he used the whites.

In this aloof manner, the young man wandered around the dilapidated site, kicking half a brick or a seat cushion of posters—several dozen layers of big-character posters of various content stacked on top of each other and pasted together to form a cushion more durable than those made from leather hides. As the young man stopped and stood under Sun Likun's window, his regal bearing and faultless comportment made the construction workers think for once of a song that was not crude: "Chairman Mao Journeys to All Parts of Our Vast Motherland."

As soon as she saw the young man, Sun Likun put down the cigarette she had just finished rolling. She had spent her whole morning on this project, scraping out the contents of several dozen fingernail-sized cigarette butts and rolling them in paper discarded from an early draft of a self-criticism. Naturally, she was reluctant to let go of it completely, so for the time being she secreted it in her blouse pocket, intending to smoke it after the young man left. For the moment, she was unwilling to figure out why she couldn't bring herself to smoke this homemade, disgusting and unseemly cigarette in front of this twenty-something young man. She would wait until the calm of night to think about it. She would like to save the memory and savor it in years to come. The men she had been with in the past had all been good-looking; in fact, most had earned their living off their good looks. Many were her dance partners, with legs and shoulders that looked as if they were sculpted out of living rock, with eyes clear and luminous, yet vacant. By contrast, this one was not yet fully formed. He still had a fair amount of growing up to do.

The young man, standing with both hands behind his back and his legs planted wide apart, looked directly toward her. The timidity in his eyes and the light smirk on the corner of his mouth were at odds, betraying one another. He watched Sun Likun for a few minutes, then, with long paces, strode away.

On the dilapidated site the vulgar activity resumed. The construction workers again started picking up cigarette butts for Sun Likun. One of them unearthed the barely smoked cigarette the young man had dropped on the ground. It had been stamped into the soft mud by the young man's steel-toed boots, so the worker had to dig for a while with his fingertips before he unearthed it. One of the others who saw it said in awe, "It's Great China brand!"

The next day, the young man appeared again. The workers had started calling him "wool suit" behind his back. He still had the air of someone just passing through. That day Sun Likun had not put on her old perennial, the completely threadbare denim work shirt. Instead, she had changed into a fine sea blue sweater. Even though the sleeves had unraveled into a ball of jumbled yarn, the sweater still gave her body a bit of a curved profile.

The young man was riding a racing bike, its entire frame an oily metallic black without a hint of color or decoration. The workers gasped in admiration at this bike, regretting that such a sleek mount didn't have a pretty saddle. Had it been up to them, they would have draped it in red and green, coiling two pounds of colored plastic cord around it! The young man remained astride his bicycle with one foot on a pedal and the other on the ground for support. Everyone noticed how his broad pants legs were tucked into his short leather boots, lending just a touch of jauntiness to his clean-cut appearance. He lifted his hand to the brim of his cap and pushed it back, revealing pitch black hair underneath. He was wearing a snow white pair of gloves and used a snow white finger to adjust the brim of his cap. The gesture gave him a dignified but paradoxical air: a commander who still smelled of his mother's milk. From that time on, that pose—the index finger raised to the brim of his hat—stuck in Sun Likun's eyes, so that whenever she would close them, it would replicate itself everywhere, again and again to the point of her exhaustion.

That day, the young man's eyes and Sun Likun's met. Just like the headlights of two cars winding toward each other along a narrow mountain road, both with a premonition of rolling over and falling into the abyss at the side of the road, yet neither yielding to the other, neither extinguishing its lights, and if they both fall into the abyss, then so be it. The construction workers saw the beautiful snake-woman inside her awaken from its hibernation and come squirming forth to the surface. Her two eyes appeared as if recharged.

Behind the young man, a thirtyish construction worker sang while urinating in the sand pit:

Who cares if it's a piece of shit
As long as it's got Omega on it!

The young man turned back and hissed, "Filthy beast." His sound was soft, his words a well-enunciated Standard Beijing Mandarin.

They all racked their brains to figure out what he had said. They all knew the words "filthy beast" but couldn't recognize them immediately in this antiseptic-sounding Beijing accent. "What's this 'filthy beast' you're talking about?" someone demanded.

"Not you, certainly. You're not worthy to be called a filthy beast," the young man replied coolly. Every syllable was enunciated clearly and completely, just as if spoken by a radio announcer at the Central People's Broadcasting Station. Only well-brushed teeth could produce such crisp words and such pure exemplary intonation.

The construction worker at the sandpit bent over, grabbed a large chunk of sandstone in one hand and made as if to pitch it, grenade-like, at the young man. The young man remained completely motionless. His thin single-fold eyelids narrowed. "Try it," he said slowly.

The construction worker dropped the chunk of stone he was holding and picked up another. This one was glistening with urine and was even hotter and heavier. Again he struck a pose as if to hurl it, yet he stepped back almost imperceptibly.

"If you make one move, you won't be here tomorrow. Try it," the young man said.

THE UNTOLD STORY, Part 1

After several weeks, as autumn turned to winter, Sun Likun was about to forget the young man whom the construction workers had dubbed "wool suit." She was a bit panicked, a bit anxious. She feared that if she forgot him, she would no longer have anything good to think about. If she forgot him, her heart would no longer have any good place. In the past, her heart had been filled only with good places, but now there wasn't a single one left. Either she had lost them or they had lost her. After all, her heart was not that big, and too many men had wanted to occupy it. She didn't have room for all of them; all she could do was constantly lose some. She didn't know what the men did after they'd been discarded by her, or what they said about her. Even if she had known, she wouldn't have quarreled with them. Men loved her beauty, loved the seductive but spiteful look in her eyes, loved her dancer's breast, loved her long neck, sharp chin and shoulders that sloped like flowing waters. Loved her picture with Zhou Enlai. They loved everything about her, except herself. And what was herself? Apart from her dancing, would she exist? She had never thought about this question before: she had made a living from her dancing, and while making a living, she didn't analyze what "living" really was. Her fingertips, the tips of her toes, the silk of her eyebrows and the ends of her hair all poured forth feeling. Yet her brain was a blank, lagging far behind her emotions.

Her heart was depleted of good places. All were gone. The most glorious ones went first. The way the leaders would walk up to her taking great bowlegged strides, shake her hand in their own warm dry hands or else—presuming upon her youth—pull her braids or pat her on the head. She had completely forgotten this. Or the time she descended from the international train, the trophy she held to her breast distinguishing her in the crowd, and a troop of Young Pioneers came rushing up to her and gave her crepe paper flowers. . . She had lost this memory without a trace.

Her heart did retain some places that were not so nice, like the time another bicycle bumped into hers, knocked her over, and mud covered half her face. When she got up, camouflaged by mud and rain slicker, she cursed the other cyclist with "Fuck your ancestors," and went on to describe in the most graphic language what his fore-fathers must necessarily have done to produce such numerous descendants. A little sound came piping up out of the crowd: "That's Sun Likun." When she turned to find the perpetrator, she saw a little girl about ten years old. The little girl's eyes looked at her as if seeing a venerated statue of Buddha toppled from its pedestal. The girl's eyes were filled with toppled veneration. The little girl was the last remnant from her past that Sun Likun would forget completely.

Just about the time Sun Likun's memory of that morning in early winter when the young man had appeared below her window had finally faded, one of her teenage girl wardens came in pointing her nightstick like a shotgun.

"Sun Likun, someone's coming to see you. Make yourself halfway presentable. He's on his way up!"

At that moment, Sun Likun could not be bothered with the girl guard's exhortations. Sun Likun's eyes were filled with tears. She had been smoking a self-rolled cigarette, when suddenly she had rushed to the window, opened it with a slap and yelled at the construction workers, "Fucking bastards. . .!"

As soon as they saw her red eyes and nose, they broke out laughing with loud hoots. They had stuffed some anti-mosquito incense into this last batch of cigarette butts they had given her.

"Sun Likun, get serious! Beijing has sent someone to investigate you." The girl guard used her nightstick to pound the termite-pocked floor. With her Sichuan intonation drawing the sounds out languidly, she said, "In-VES-ti-gate!" like a satisfying yawn. "From the Central Government!"

"I'm COM-ing!" Sun Likun replied from inside her face towel as she wiped away the residue of the mosquito repellant. The towel, stiff from filth, skittered about on the wire clothesline that bisected her room. She hocked and blew a wad of mucus, then used the ramrod-stiff towel to polish her face. When she looked up from her towel, she remained motionless.

The young man in the woolen suit stood facing her, his hands behind his back. Behind him were layer upon layer of faded stage backdrops. As he saw her face rise out of the darkness of the dirty towel, he gazed at her with a mixture of revulsion and pity. Suddenly it occurred to her that in all her thirty-four years, her face had never been as naked as at this moment. Then she realized that she was standing by the backdrop of Broken Bridge from *The Legend of White Snake*. The light gray stone of the bridge had become permeated with its dismal history.

She didn't know what she murmured, whether it was an apology or an excuse. She turned and walked into another corner of the scenery. It was a completely unceremonious exit. In all of Sun Likun's dance career, there was only one other time when she had made such an exit. That time, as soon as she had gone on stage, she realized she had forgotten to put on a slip. She knew that once the unrelenting stage lights beat down on her, she would appear practically naked. Back then, she had improvised and, with a turn, had walked offstage. But this time, she didn't even know the reason for her improvised exit. Such a young man as this, appearing on such an absurd deserted stage as hers. Such unexpectedness, such a huge blunder, unforeseen and yet clearly discernible in the darkness— these things had compelled her to exit her stage, leaving the young man suspended in an awkward intermission of time and space. The abrupt exit greatly surprised even herself. She retreated into a corner beyond the reach of his eyesight, not to adjust her clothes or her hair, but rather to change completely her bearing and attitude.

She knew her appearance and comportment were unspeakably vile, like the sight of an unbearably ugly naked body. She gazed blindly from the shade of the corner, unable to find a suitable state of mind or facial expression. She stood there until the intermission could be drawn out no longer. The room's silence already seemed like the racket of gongs and cymbals in a suspense scene in Chinese opera. She could sense the young man's discomfort and annoyance at the empty stage and feel him sizing up the entire scene during this awkward interlude: the cigarette rolled from newspaper that lay extinguished on the windowsill; the wire clothesline that bisected the room diagonally, draped with the withered vines of her brassieres, underwear and stockings; the congealed leftovers; and that flowery chamberpot. She could feel him, catlike, without sound or motion, sizing up everything.

When she finally stepped out of her corner and walked on stage again, she was completely transformed. A mysterious change had taken place in that darkness. She was still wearing the sea blue sweater, its sleeves a tangle of unraveled threads. It still stretched grotesquely taut across her bosom, which had long since spread out abundantly. She was still wearing that same pair of pants with the part around the knees protruding forward, making her seem as if she were eternally kneeling. Yet she was a completely different person from before her hasty exit. That chin of hers, now thick and broad, once again floated freely, drawing exquisite arcs in the air. Her face was still a pallid white from being kept in humidity and darkness, yet her deportment revealed her inherent beauty, which resurged on her long slender neck like some kind of ache. She shrank away from this ache while tentatively raising her head. Under her skin, from somewhere deep inside her bones, her snakelike suppleness and coiled splendor had revived—accompanied by a snake's cold radiance and proud aloofness.

The young man, who had found himself a seat and lit a cigarette, saw the change that had come over her as soon as she walked out toward him. He stood up without realizing it.

The girl guard, thoroughly flushed, brought in a thermos bottle with bamboo wicker shell and, addressing the young man as "Commissar," said that the water was freshly boiled and the tea was specially sent over from the deputy troupe leader's office. Sichuan is known for three famous products, the girl continued: pickled mustard roots, five-grain spirits and Happy Mountain green tea. We hope the Commissar will be understanding: no matter how many times you wash the teacup, you can never get rid of the film. Thus apologizing, she poured the young man a cup of tea. Don't call me commissar, he said. We've all come here from the ends of the earth. My surname is Xu.

The teenage girl bowed her head obediently, addressing him as Commissar Xu.

Xu Qunshan. Qun as in *qunzhong,* "the masses," he said; *shan* (mountain) as in "the mountains and the rivers of the Motherland." His voice was not strong. Like himself, it was light and elegant.

By now the teenage girl had caught a glimpse of the transformed Sun Likun who had walked out of the corner . . . but it was beyond her comprehension what had caused Sun Likun to become attractive again.

When only the two of them were left alone again, he removed his white gloves, finger by finger, revealing extremely smooth cuticles. She had never seen such smooth flawless fingers on a man. As the workmen down below sang ". . .the Street Committee is standing her guard for us, the Party Branch Office is chatting her up for us," neither turned to look. A dirt clod came sailing through the window and landed on the table, crumbling benignly and scattering all over it. He merely turned his head to look at the dirt. Then she looked at it, too, with fuller knowledge. She was in the habit of sitting cross-legged on the tabletop to feel the cool breeze, chatting mindlessly with the construction workers. Soon she and the men would be calling each other names and throwing things at each other. But now this seemed a childish intrusion.

She stood up, closed the window and wiped the table. Meanwhile, he asked questions and she responded, both using a stilted form of language, barely talking at all. She returned to her chair and sat down, and he asked her the year in which she had won the international prize. Nineteen fifty-eight, she answered. She noticed that his fingertips moved as he listened to her brief account. The subtle annoyance they betrayed somehow obstructed her from making her oft-told "confession" a bit livelier. The nervousness in his fingertips made her feel the weight of his worries, his tepid disdain and fault-finding toward everything. When she came to her tryst with that foreign devil of a dancer, he was just placing his snow white gloves on the table. Suddenly he had a change of heart, picked them up again and sat there frowning slightly, as if he did not know what to do with them.

She looked into his eyes. She thought something was very much out of place. Never before had she seen a man with such eyes who looked at her in such a way.

"Don't call me commissar. Just use my name." With his full and mellow Beijing accent he interrupted her account, or repentance, as well as her gaze. "Call me Xu Qunshan." He handed her a cigarette. At first she didn't understand such civilized language. Such a set of fingers, speaking such civilized language. She didn't know what to say. Now it was his turn to gaze at her.

THE OFFICIAL ACCOUNT, Part 2
Memorandum to the Responsible Comrades of the Propaganda, Culture, and Education Department of Sichuan Province

After receiving your instructions of April 8 (document no. 00700016), our troupe immediately convened a meeting of Party members and cadres to pass on the information. Everyone was deeply moved that our beloved and respected premier, loaded with cares and working his heart out on important affairs of state, would concern himself with an ordinary performer. Immediately after the meeting we opened an inquiry into Xu Qunshan. Everyone shared the recollection of having harbored doubts toward this self-proclaimed "special envoy" from the very beginning. In particular, the female members of the Vigilance Committee who carried out the guard duty voiced their skepticism concerning this individual's background. They expressed to the Party organization their resolve to exhaust their entire strength in assisting to clear up the causes of Sun Likun's illness. The evidence they have gathered is as follows:

On November 20, this fellow Xu entered Sun Likun's room for the first time and spent two hours and ten minutes alone with her. According to accounts, unusual sounds were heard emanating from her room.

Thereafter, this Xu fellow spent two to two and a half hours alone with Sun Likun every day. Obviously, during this time an illicit man-woman relationship developed between them.

On December 26, this Xu, driving a military motorcycle, carried Sun off, and the two spent a total of six or seven hours alone together. According to testimony, Xu and Sun cohabited at the Provincial Party Committee's guesthouse, engaging in at least five hours of licentious activities.

On December 28, the Leadership Committee unanimously passed a resolution to order a gynecological examination of Sun. Sun repeatedly refused to cooperate, so the female members of the Vigilance Committee had no choice but forcefully to conduct Sun to the obstetrics and gynecology ward of the Provincial People's Hospital. The results of the examination were that Sun's hymen is fully eliminated, but at this time it could not be ascertained conclusively whether Sun had had sexual relations with Xu.

We conclude this letter by conveying our highest revolutionary salute!

Sichuan Province Performing Arts Troupe
Revolutionary Leadership Committee
April 10, 1972

THE POPULAR ACCOUNT, Part 2

Actually, the girls guarding Sun Likun only thought of all those outlandish things after the incident happened. It was only after Xu Qunshan disappeared without a trace that they thought back in detail about the whole chain of events. In their recollections, they all vied with each other, each trying to claim that it was she who first spotted Xu Qunshan's "fox's tail." They said that from the very beginning they sensed his furtiveness; that he had some motive he couldn't reveal to anyone; that he had inner qualities totally at odds with his apparently reasonable temperament, his completely anachronistic appearance and demeanor, and his civility. They didn't use this last word, because civility was a word with too obscure a meaning, obscure to the point of containing a hint of approval. They turned a blind eye to what had been their actual experience: they were enchanted by that air of civility, thoroughly and impardonably enchanted. It was only much later that they really thought about Xu Qunshan's unreasonable elegance. He didn't belong to their society or their era—"our great and glorious era," as they called it. Either he belonged to the past or else to the future. But it was only after the incident that they took a deep breath and realized all this. By then it had already happened: Sun Likun's intimate secrets had quietly tortured her until, one early morning at year's end, she had lost her mind.

It was only after Sun Likun was committed to Chongqing's Joyous Song Mountain Mental Hospital that the girl guards really thought through everything that was unusual or illogical. When they took a breath of cold air and stated that from the very beginning, they had the feeling that Sun Likun was being lured into a trap, they were lying. If they had really been aware of Xu Qunshan's enticing trap from the very beginning, it would have meant that they had fallen into it themselves, harboring only a tiny bit of skepticism along with their willingness. When it was already far too late, deep in their hearts they recognized this. They also silently recognized that Xu Qunshan's completely alien presence had infected each one of them in some absurd way, making them suddenly de-emphasize the thick arms and legs and loud voices of which they had thought themselves so proud.

The results of the inquiry were as could be expected. The leadership of the Performing Arts Troupe communicated all the way up the chain of command, and finally they determined there was no such person as Xu Qunshan. Now they could see the logic of the circumstances surrounding Sun Likun's breakdown: Xu Qunshan had gained her emotions and her body by deception, and after gaining them, dumped it all like dirt. As for what had really happened, Sun Likun herself uttered not a word. If you asked her, if you coaxed her, all she would do was laugh sorrowfully and stupidly. It was the kind of laughter that could only come from someone with a shattered heart.

The teenage girls pooled all their recollections of the affair, freely filling in many asides and details. They remembered that as soon as Xu Qunshan would come to do that thing with Sun Likun, the cell door would be locked up and sealed tight, and the two of them would cover up every crack with the *People's Daily*. When the girls had used a hairpin to pierce through the door seam, the next day it was pasted over with a layer of pages from *Red Flag*. But *none* of them brought up a certain trifling detail: each time Xu Qunshan came, he would pull out of his pocket a chocolate bar wrapped in gold foil, give it to the girl guard on duty and tell her, "There's no need to stand guard here." The teenage girls had never encountered such exquisite chocolate. It seemed like something commissioned for the imperial court. They had heard that ballet queen Ulyanova ate just one small square of chocolate every day and nothing else. The chocolate she ate must have been exactly like this.

"It's really quite simple," the most insightful of the girls spoke up, the short one who always wrote the big-character posters. "Sun Likun is just a slut. She can't get along without a man. Don't you all remember? When there was no man around, she started jabbering away with those construction workers down below. As soon as Xu Qunshan started to seduce her, of *course* he succeeded. The tragic part is that this time Sun Likun felt real emotions. Think about it: you've lost your fame, have no family and no longer have anything to be proud of. So naturally it's not like before when she could fool around with people and *their* emotions. This time Sun Likun gave everything she had and gave it to someone who was toying with her. It's that simple."

When the young leader of the Performing Arts Troupe heard the short guard present this thorough summation, he knit his eyebrows and nodded his head for a while. After a moment the deputy director, a former dancer who had been crippled in a dancing accident, said, "Our Venerable Premier Zhou's secretary has written again, saying that if the Joyous Song Mountain nuthouse can't cure Sun Likun, then we're supposed to send her to Shanghai. Let's see if the finance department can't come up with enough to get Sun Likun two woolen outfits, something presentable. And get her hair done. Aren't there some underground beauty parlors now that perm women's hair? How can Sun Likun be shown to anybody in her present state, halfway between human and ghost? Not only would we lose face for the two hundred or so people in our troupe; we'd also lose face for all eighty million people of Sichuan Province! If the premier's secretary ever happened to visit her at the hospital in Shanghai, he'd think we'd been abusing her! He'd also say we've been squandering talent!"

Later on, we heard the premier's secretary actually *did* go to Shanghai and saw an essentially recovered Sun Likun. Sun Likun posed for a photograph for our province's newspaper, and the paper ran it. The look in her eyes was no longer that seductive venomous look. Her fierce aspect was gone. Her smile was proper and correct. She appeared more normal than ever, more so than before her illness.

It is said that, while in Shanghai, Sun Likun had a frequent visitor at her side, or rather a constant companion. It was a young woman. The doctors and nurses knew her as one of Sun Likun's fans from her performing days.

THE UNTOLD STORY, Part 2

Saturday, May 11, 1963
Weather clear

At 5:30 AM I ran with my classmates to the door of the theater. When I saw the big wooden "sold out" sign hanging in the box office, I was so disappointed. Actually, all of us have seen it once except for me. I've seen it five times. It's *so good!*

A sedan drove up and stopped at the door of the theater. We were all about to leave when we realized that it was the performers who were getting out of the car! Their Sichuan dialect really sounded cute! I thought it was really lovely. So we stood on the steps as they entered the theater and watched them talking and laughing and gesturing. I recognized the actor who played Xu Xian. I wouldn't have imagined his nose was so big!

The last one to step out of the car was White Snake. None of us spoke; we just stood there staring at her. She was taller than the other actresses, and her back was so straight that it seemed to lean backwards a bit. She was wearing a pair of wide black harem pants and an India red woolen blouse. The collar almost trailed down to her shoulders. She was so beautiful. How is it possible for a person to be so beautiful?! (While writing that line, I blushed—my face is so hot!) Her long, long neck went all the way down, exposing her cleavage. She reminded me of a statue! Her bosom is really beautiful, like you'd see on a heroine in distress. It stands straight up. I'd really like to touch her, to see if it is sculpted or real. I frighten myself when I have thoughts like that.

Oh, yes. Her shoes had a buckle undone, and the metallic sound of the buckle followed her every step, giving off a very light "ding, ding!" military-attack sound. No one was supposed to hear this sound, but everyone was so quiet, just looking at her, speechless.

Why is it that I'm always writing about this stuff in my diary the past few days? I've always liked dance, but since I saw her dancing, I feel I don't like dance so much as I like the body that produces the dance. So am I strange? Can anyone tell me if I am normal?

Mama tells me I'm not a very normal child. She says it in a way that makes it sound like she's praising me. I do so hope that I'm normal, that I'm just like everyone else, otherwise I'll be so isolated! I'm so scared!

But what about my classmates, Little Plum and Lili? Weren't they dumbfounded too when they saw White Snake? I'll bet they're just as infatuated with her as I am, that they think about touching her body. They just wouldn't admit it. I wouldn't admit it to them, either. I have to lock up this diary. No one must see it.

When I look at my body now that I've started puberty, I think of White Snake's. My body is so pitiful. Someday can I grow up to look like her?

Saturday, May 18, 1963
Rainy day

Lili and the girls and I waited and waited, but nobody turned in any tickets. This was the last performance—we *had* to get in!

Suddenly White Snake appeared before us. She was already in makeup, and her eyelashes looked like a feathered fan. She seemed as if she were about to meet someone. After a couple of minutes, she glanced at her watch and was getting ready to go inside when a man ran up to her, and the two of them shook hands vigorously. I don't know who started it, but all seven or eight of us started pleading, "Auntie White Snake, please take us in with you!" Again and again we besieged her, calling out like this. She paid no attention to us. When she was about to walk inside, she turned to us and smiled, saying "I can only take one of you." Her Sichuan dialect sounded so pretty, with a rounded vowel on the word "one." She looked over our seven or eight faces and pointed to me, saying, "You were very well behaved just now. You didn't call out. I'm taking you inside!"

My friends all turned on me, telling her I'd seen it five times already. But she chose me anyway.

She took me backstage. When her eyes spotted my watch, they widened as she said, "Such a young boy and already wearing a wristwatch!"

I replied, "I'm not a boy."

She took a hard look at me and said, "Then why is your hair so short? Is it for swimming?" I couldn't think of anything to say.

She let me go find a spot on my own from where I could watch the performance, since she had to get into costume. I hid behind a side-curtain for a while until somebody yelled at me to leave. Finally I found an empty seat in the last row of the audience. Onstage they had just performed up to the part where White Snake and Blue Snake start their battle. Blue Snake tries to woo White Snake, and they are determined to test each other in battle. If Blue Snake wins, White Snake will marry him, and if White Snake wins, Blue Snake will become a female and serve White Snake all her life. Blue Snake is defeated, and as soon as the stage lights go dark, then light up again, he has already become a female. After becoming a female, Blue Snake is so loyal and brave, so attentive toward White Snake even in the smallest matters. What if he had not become a female? Wouldn't White Snake then have avoided having anything to do with that idiot Xu Xian? I really can't stand Xu Xian! If it hadn't been for him, White Snake would not have suffered such tribulations. If it hadn't been for that detestable Xu Xian, White Snake and Blue Snake certainly would have been very happy together. Oh, it really gets under my skin!

Starting tomorrow, I will not think about White Snake any more. How is it that I even see her in my dreams? What's happening to me? Exams are coming up soon. I have to remember, I belong to the successor generation of Communism. I have to be normal and healthy to be a worthy successor.

THE UNTOLD STORY, Part 3

With two fingers Xu Qunshan drew a pack of cigarettes out of his pocket, Great China brand. With his sharp slender little finger, he lifted off the sealing band, then the tinfoil. He suddenly lowered his face and smelled the cigarettes. Sun Likun took the cigarette he handed her, put it between her lips, and seeing him flick his cigarette lighter, quickly brought her face over to him, then, from up close, stole a look in his eyes.

He began to speak about her dancing. "When I was very young, I once saw you dance." He didn't say whether he thought it was good or bad. That was many years ago, he said. She interrupted, saying that was another lifetime. For a long time he said nothing, then, "You are still like that. You haven't changed."

"I *have* changed," she replied.

"You really haven't," he countered. "I recognized you the first moment I laid eyes on you." In his heart he thought, even though you have nothing else left, neither status, shape, youth nor self-respect. He said, "I recognized you as soon as I saw you that day when I was standing under your window." He smiled, then coughed slightly.

She was infatuated with the way he coughed: one hand balled into an empty fist placed tightly on his lips. His innate vulnerability and tenderness were suddenly revealed in that cough. She could no longer remember who, these days, could cough so elegantly.

"What do you want to investigate about me?"

"I cannot tell you at this time."

"I don't know what there is about me for anyone to investigate." She pouted her lips slightly. Years ago she used to bowl men over with that lovely innocent look. But she could see no reaction on his part. "Is there something to investigate?" she asked. She shifted her entire weight to one leg and stretched out the other leg, her toes pointed tightly. Before his eyes, the leg rose up, and after a moment it no longer resembled a leg. It seemed as if it could be extended infinitely, so pliant and tough it was. An incredible life reawakened and unfolded in that leg. With its own soul and body, it made those shapeless pants suddenly appear to have vanished. "What could I have that could be worthy of your investigating?" she asked languidly. "A dancer who left home and entered dancing school at age ten, who, when it was time to write letters home, had to walk the dormitory corridor a dozen times or so and grab somebody, hunting for words: how do you write this or that character? Without any education, how could I have any counter-revolutionary thought? I, who while writing the self-criticism and the confession, pored over the whole dog-eared dictionary. If I hadn't written them, I never would have learned so many characters." She said this while watching her leg hover in the air. "I was always harder on myself than the other dancers. When I was just ten, I'd tie one leg on the bedpost before I'd go to sleep. If the other girls were trying to do splits to look like 'a quarter of three,' I was doing them to look like 'ten after ten.' You see, that bitterly hard training all grew into this leg and cannot be removed." She looked at her leg like a mother gazing at her beautiful but deformed child.

"Why didn't you ever marry?" he suddenly asked.

"Haven't married yet," she corrected, looking at him but not trying to probe his motives. He remained silent, so she prattled on. "I had no childhood, no adolescence. My childhood was one piece of candy split five ways. No money and afraid of getting fat."

"So you were never in love with anyone?"

"Well, actually I was once." She bowed her head and looked at her other leg and spoke again: "I don't know. You want me to give explanations for all that?"

He told her just to talk freely. It shouldn't necessarily be like an interrogator with the interrogated. I'm not looking to find fault. He looked at her other leg. It also had its own mind and will. It shot forward a few times, then made circles a few times, hinting at a mute language. He looked on, stupefied.

She watched him looking at her. "I really don't know what there is to investigate." She smiled, revealing a delicate and complete set of teeth, naturally sparkling.

His motionless hands already held their third cigarette. The cigarette burned by itself like temple incense; he hardly smoked it. Section after white section of ash dropped into the clay dish below his hand; it was the one in which she kept her chili paste. The paste had dried up, leaving a few deep red traces. The room was full of similar evidence of a person with no emotional life, living a life without emotion.

"I've read your file," he said.

"You saw those things I wrote? All four hundred pages? They let you see them?" She flushed red, and the red deepened. She lowered her leg, and the expressiveness of her two legs vanished almost completely.

He said he had. He didn't say that those four hundred pages constantly covered the same ground. Again and again, each time revealing just a bit more detail. The Committee had wanted her to talk about every little trifle. About the time she indulged in a full three days of debauchery with that Soviet dancer: which one of them undid the trouser waistband first. People felt it was very important to get to the bottom of this, because whoever had undone his trousers first influenced major affairs of state, perhaps determining which nation would trespass on which nation's border. Because Sun Likun, try as she might, could not recall who was first and who was second, she had been locked up these past two years, so the Committee had told young Commissar Xu. And then, when the hostilities began on the Sino-Soviet border, Sun Likun's situation became even more serious, because she came under suspicion of being a Soviet-trained spy. After that, whether she was the first to undo her pants was by far the least of her transgressions.

She said to Xu, "Our Motherland sent me to represent the Chinese people, and he was sent to represent the Soviet people. The two of us danced a *pas de deux*. For three days and three nights we were rehearsing that dance. I don't know how it . . . this affair, how to explain it? Do you think you could explain it?" She looked at young Commissar Xu, who stared back with the perplexity of the unworldly.

After leaving her, Xu Qunshan repeatedly thought about her way of expressing herself. Though an emotionally mature woman, Sun had an intellect that had not developed past childhood. Her emotions were outside of her consciousness, accustomed to spilling out of their own accord. When she described her tryst, step by step, it was like a description of a scene in which she was acting: she put her whole heart and body into it. Even though sometimes she improvised a little, in fact most of her movements were choreographed. She did not realize she had choreographed her entire reality, her whole material existence. She had allowed her feelings and her hopes to dance. Dance has only intuition and inference; it is a language beyond language. Early mankind had dance before language; although unfathomable, at the same time dance contains the most fundamental precision. In Sun Likun's body, brimming with dance, he had unearthed that completely forgotten precision. This discovery excited and moved him. In the face of that precision beyond language, all knowledge, all defined emotions appeared too obtuse, too concrete.

Intuition and inference had become incarnate in her dancer's body, a body that regardless of its pose or contortions still contained that basic precise expression. Xu Qunshan knew that people instinctively loved this body, but their love was too concrete, too purposeful. Her body's lack of concreteness kept it ever beyond their grasp, so they took revenge by loving it more. In an instant, Xu Qunshan understood clearly the origin of his childhood fascination with her. Xu Qunshan loved that body; he did not seek the underlying meaning of its insinuations, because the most fundamentally *precise* language was to be found in those insinuations: it could not be pursued further.

THE UNTOLD STORY, Part 4

March 31, 1970
Village X, Shanxi Province
    When I got up this morning, the *kang* had long since grown cold. All there is in the cistern is a suspension of muddy yellowish-brown water. I've been drinking this yellowish-brown paste for half a year now. I'm damn sick of it.

I went to draw water. From the very beginning the villagers have never helped me. They helped those two girl students from Taiyuan draw water, plotting the day when they would draw them into their huts and onto their *kangs*. They wouldn't think of drawing *me* in. When the foreman of the Production Brigade tells me to go repair the terraced paddies, there's no "meaningful look" in his eyes. Oh, spare me! I've got to get my hair cut a little shorter. That way both the foreman and the brigade cadres will have even fewer "meaningful looks" for me. Now wouldn't *that* be a tremendous convenience!

I refuse to mend the terraced paddies. More fundamentally, I refuse to "mend the earth." I've got to get a doctor's excuse that I've got a swollen liver, spleen, lymph node or whatever.

I've still got to go out, still have to get something to eat. I ate two pieces of cold yams left over from yesterday. They were chilled through and through. I flipped through my clothes looking for something to wear. I found that woolen military school uniform my eldest brother gave me as a going-away present. I put it on, donned the cap and turned around a couple of times in my hut. That won't do; I've got to go draw water again.

When I went out the door wearing that uniform yesterday, I ran into Xiaolian. She asked me straight out when I was leaving. Joining the army? As a special soldier? From the looks of that uniform, you're not going to be just your average soldier!

I'm leaving tomorrow, I said.

Li Xiaolian was so envious her nose turned red. She said to me from this moment on you won't have to mend the earth any more. If she had been able to get a hold of a uniform like that, she would have paraded all over the village, accepting accolades. She said, you little thing, you, you sure can keep a secret. When you get your outstanding soldier medal, don't forget to have a big picture taken and send it back to us.

Certainly, I replied.

After you join the army, she continued, Zhang Ping and I are going to be the only Intellectual Youth left here. I reflected that if I didn't leave, it would still be just the two of you. Whenever the brigade leader and the party secretary extend an invitation to eat pig's head meat and drink twice-distilled sorghum liquor, it is always only the two of you at the *kang* table.

After I drew two and a half buckets of muddy water and went back to my hut, all the people I ran into going about their work said hey, it's great to be a soldier, and it's a real honor when they give you a woolen uniform so soon after you join.

Is it just as simple as that? When I put the cover of *Red Flag* on top of one of my old movie magazines, then what I was reading became *Red Flag*. When I put the cover of *Quotations of Chairman Mao* over my copy of *Les Misérables*, then it became *Quotations of Chairman Mao*. A woolen military uniform immediately transforms me into a first-class, high-level person, receiving everyone's admiration as a wool-clad special soldier. It's going to be hard to step down from such a pedestal. I can shed this uniform tomorrow, but I won't be able to shed the lie.

I must go. Let them see me march right out of this village forever in that woolen uniform.

I must go back to Beijing. Let the lie have a bigger stage.

April 2, 1970
On the train to Beijing

Packing. It's just like a warrior departing, never to return. Everybody in the village came by to collect my castoff things. While they sifted through them, they told me how wonderful it is to be a soldier, what zest it brings to one's life.

I let them take all my stuff. All I've kept are my books and magazines. I just can't stand the thought of them using the pages of *Les Misérables* on the latrine as toilet paper, or to patch their windows with, or to make embroidery patterns for their cloth shoes. I can't stand the thought of them pasting that faded stage photo of White Snake onto their mud walls, calling her a "bewitching she-devil." I have to take it with me. Ever since I was twelve, wherever I've gone, I've taken White Snake with me.

When the train arrived at Dingxiang, a lot of people got on. I steadfastly refused to open my eyes, letting the country folk think I was sleeping the sleep of the dead. Nevertheless, somebody jostled me, saying Elder Brother, look at that lady, already eight months pregnant.

First time anybody's ever called me "Elder Brother." Just like *Red Flag* or *Quotations of Chairman Mao,* it's what's on the outside that counts; the seeds don't betray the fruit. I'm nineteen, and this is the first time I have felt that my body is inherently androgynous. Ever since I was little, I have been fond of cutting my hair short and wearing hand-me-down clothes from my elder brothers, which others viewed as, if not abnormal, then at least unusual. That's just fine with me. A purely feminine girl is both silly and insipid.

Actually, people who knew me saw me as a girl, and strangers saw me as a boy. It was my neither-male-nor-femaleness during the time when I was "mending the earth" that made my life much more convenient and much safer. And afforded me much more respect. Being addressed as "Elder Brother" opened a strange and wondrous door for me. A door that led to unlimited possibilities.

Will I be able to find my way through these possibilities? Is there a destiny that transcends the dichotomy of male and female? Despite having a body with a uterus and ovaries, is it possible that I am not without a choice?

I despise the superficiality of girls.

I scorn the vulgarity of boys.

How tedious I am. How bizarre I am. As I quite naturally stood to offer my place to the pregnant woman, I felt queasiness toward her mottled face.

The train rumbled on, and I had nothing else to do but rummage through the books I'd brought in my luggage. My eyes stopped on that photo of White Snake. Always looking back with that insolent expression. I wonder where you are now?

THE UNTOLD STORY, Part 5

That day Sun Likun turned the light on at two in the afternoon. On winter afternoons the light in the scenery warehouse became so faint that all objects lost their shadows. She would pull the cord of the naked lightbulb down to the appropriate height and let the light faithfully project her body's shadow onto a whitewashed stage backdrop. Without a mirror, she could only use her shadow projection to groom herself. She had been doing this for almost a month and saw her body slimming down and her figure becoming more defined. She was once again her lithe slender self. For weeks she had been secretly groping her way out of bed in the middle of the night and practicing dance. Now from the shadow projection she could see that dance had completely returned to her body. All of the surplus fat had been trimmed off, and her knifelike will had repeatedly sculpted her form. She slowly reviewed her dance movements, taking a few tentative "snake steps." On the whitewashed stage backdrop a spring snake was reviving after a long hibernation, limbering up to freshness and new life.

In her thirty-four years of life, this was the first time she felt that the most comforting part about being together with a man was not his body but his heart. Yet the comfort brought with it some anxiety, feelings of inadequacy, even a bit of despair. Xu Qunshan would come to this place every day for one or two hours. Gradually she had come to understand that his investigation was of a completely different nature. Or perhaps its nature had changed in midcourse; it was no longer an investigation *per se*. They would exchange a few words together, then sit side by side on the table, their backs to the window. Outside the window there had long since been no flirting choruses of "I've seen thousands of pretty girls." Those were not the kind of songs one sings to a tightly shuttered window and to a famous dancer whose renewed elevation had left them all in the dust.

He would just sit there with a lit cigarette, watching her take off her quilted cotton outer garments, molting them layer by layer until her form was finally revealed. He would watch her gradually begin to stir, gradually begin to dance. As he explained to her repeatedly, this was an important component of the investigation.

Her intuition told her that the investigation had a completely different purpose. She felt as if he had come to rescue her, taking measures that were completely unfathomable to her. Yet she couldn't penetrate this young man's aloofness and politeness to discover his true mission. Sometimes she felt as if this storeroom stuffed with scenery had organized itself into a play and the wiry young man had become a character in it. She never considered whether he might be toying with her or whether he might be infatuated with her; she only felt that he was very different. She could no longer be without him, no matter who he was, even if the purpose of his existence was to torment her, to destroy her bit by bit with his cultivated manner.

She asked him straight out, "Who do you have at home? Parents, sisters, brothers?"

He answered her straight out, saying: "I have them all. I'm the youngest. Both of my elder brothers are honor students at the Harbin Military Institute of Technology. My older and younger sisters aren't worth mentioning. I have everything: money, power, books, status. Would you believe I even have a pistol? You name it, I've got it. I can play the piano and the flute. I tore off all the padding around the hammers behind the piano keys so it sounds really ancient. I like to read *Das Kapital* and Byron. Mao Zedong's poetry is nicely written. Some of his most opinionated commentaries are his most wonderful, full of the force of his personality. They're especially humorous. Now do you know who I am?" The light coming in through the window outlined the shoulders of his immaculate military overcoat in its squarish arrogance.

"You're. . .twenty?"

"Twenty," he laughed. "The sun at eight in the morning."

"So young, and already a special envoy from the Central Government, " she said, suppressing any feeling of suspicion.

"My brain is not young." He tapped his cigarette ash.

"You must have a lot of girlfriends."

"I've had very few girlfriends."

She was still dancing as she talked. Half her life she had talked in this manner, otherwise she felt her talk was completely incoherent. She had stripped down to a tight nylon dance leotard riddled with tiny holes. Her neck and legs pirouetted, describing an incredible spiral. All of the scenery backdrops in the room had come to life in Chengdu's mildew tide of winter. The coagulated pig's blood used as primer on the canvases had gradually dissolved in the humidity; out of the dust-covered corners, out of the forgotten abandoned darkness, wafted its penetrating odor. Xu Qunshan and Sun Likun both caught the scent of this blood coming back to life but had no desire to search out its origins. It wasn't the only odor present; there was also the odor of a body so hot it caused clothing to cling and the smell of the sweat of a dancer's feet.

These pungent odors caused Sun's rotating body gradually to be transformed, to be reborn in the role of the beautiful snake-woman. Whenever Xu Qunshan watched this metamorphosis, his enthusiasm and amazement would make him cough slightly, with a lightly clasped fist pressed to his lips, elegantly concealing any actions of his internal organs.

She said, "You're going to leave someday, and you're never coming back?"

He replied, "Tomorrow is the last day."

"The investigation is finished?" she asked.

"Finished," he said. His eyes were crystal clear and fathomless, like the deepest well. She regained her composure, standing up as she felt her whole body collapsing.

"Tomorrow is the last day," she repeated. "I'm a lot older than you," she said mindlessly.

With his leather boots making a "ga-dunk" sound, he walked straight up to her, extending his hand. She didn't know why he was extending his hand, but her intuition made her want to put her whole body into it. Nevertheless, he took her hand and said see you tomorrow. He left with wide strides, his woolen overcoat swaying, looking like some young commander-in-chief.

Throughout the whole night, she savored the warmth that the

silky feel of his hand had left with her. The soft, cool and smooth feeling of silk. She had never before touched such a fine and delicate male hand. The back of the hand, the palm, the fingers constantly in motion. She could well believe that he played the piano and the flute, with hands like those! Tomorrow is the last day. The final day.

All night she did not sleep. She had never before met a man as manly as Xu Qunshan, nor had she ever met a man as kind and amiable. Still, she knew that the last day was the last day, and she harbored no expectations at all. She recalled his every glance, every time he knit his eyebrows. Every occasional smile. How could she ever deserve a man like this? She now had no past and no future, just a lot of years and a pile of political offenses.

She fell in love with this young man in the woolen military academy uniform the eve of that final day. Her intuition had long since told her that she was not alone in this—that he had more layers of emotion, more depth than he showed. His two long black eyebrows rarely lifted in a smile, and his two hands were constantly prone to fidgeting. Gradually she became more conscious that this was not all of him, that there was more to him than that. He came here not just to carry out an in-depth investigation. He had another mission as well. Maybe it was only to get close to her. Yet he had never been like other men she had experienced, no full-bodied, nose-penetrating desire. The young man named Xu Qunshan had never, ever been like them.

On the afternoon of this last day, as she projected her shadow, the shadow was only nineteen years old. Shadows, unlike faces and complexions, do not fade. On this gray humid winter afternoon, she wanted to make herself look her best, to spend this last day well. She had slimmed down during this month. She had slimmed down so much that the teenage girls who guarded her started to get restless, started to murmur comments to each other. Day by day she underwent a metamorphosis, day by day she regained her original form. Even she was startled when she saw this perfect shadow projection: it was a shadow cast from her youth, hair bound up high and tight, creating perfect symmetry with her rising chin.

At exactly three o'clock, a knock sounded at the door. Sun Likun said come right in. Xu Qunshan was not wearing his riding boots, nor was he wearing his woolen overcoat, and at once he appeared much thinner. He was wearing a pair of corduroy cloth shoes. He walked up to her without a breath or a sound.

She trembled solemnly, her complexion a malignant white. On her upper body she wore a cardigan sweater of India red, its neckline nearly exposing her shoulders. It was old, and some portions of it were riddled with tiny moth holes. She became embarrassed about her careful primping and preening. Her age was on the surface for all to see; she was unable to hide it. She felt like the India red sweater: slightly shabby but exceptionally endearing.

"Have a seat," he said. As usual he hooked his foot around the chair's leg and pulled it over to create a normal distance between the two chairs. A proper distance conducive to self-respect.

She sat down, feeling a bit sapped of strength.

"Are you really not coming tomorrow?" she asked.

He laughed. Laughed at this terribly silly question of hers. Laughed in her hopeless despairing face.

She said, "If you would come every day, I could be locked up here forever, and I wouldn't mind."

He didn't answer, but he didn't think her words were too presumptuous or forward. He just watched his cigarette smoke swirl up like incense before her face, as he meditatively and silently savored this rare moment.

She, too, was quiet and watched the ashen-blue smoke. Watched two people's thoughts roll about in the smoke. Even hopelessness seemed to have its savor. She knew that once this silence was finished, everything would be finished. He and she, finished in the midst of this silence.

It was the kind of silence that allowed even their scattered thoughts to be heard. Even the rolling of the smoke made a sound.

The scenery backdrop covering heaven and earth gave off the raw smell of warmed-up pig's blood. Suddenly Xu Qunshan spoke up.

"When I was little, I once saw you dance."

Sun Likun was stunned. Why did he bring this up again?

"I was only eleven or twelve back then."

She thought, he's already talked about all this; why is he talking about it again?

"It was as if I were possessed," he said, then laughed as if recalling his silliness in childhood. His laugh trailed off into a sigh.

Then he fell silent, his eyelids drooping. Sensitive and proud single eye-folds. It made her love him so much her heart ached.

The silence was taut like a violin string ready to snap.

Suddenly she said, "Take me with you."

The tears in her eyes formed a reflective ring that turned back and forth. Take me with you. Her body leaned forward; her hands came to rest on her knees where they supported her sharp chin between them. She brought herself down low and raised up her face toward him. Her submissiveness was like that of a female slave. The slender delicate head she raised looked like a female snake's head. Because it took effort to raise it, a tiny group of fine wrinkles formed on her completely hairless forehead.

Xu Qunshan, his cloth shoes swinging back and forth, said, "I want to take you away."

She didn't ask him where he would take her or why. She thought, this cannot have a good outcome. In his calm even demeanor she found what she had been seeking, the thing she had been searching for all along. A plot? His thin clean face was so young, any plotting would certainly have hardened it, taken away its vitality.

He said he had already informed the leadership of the Performing Arts Troupe.

He said they had agreed. Her eyes went slack; she didn't want to see through this plot. She simply prepared to leave, taking down her unruly stiff towel from the wire clothesline and packing it along with her completely bald toothbrush and black plastic comb with white grime on the teeth. She stuffed these things into her purse, a bag purchased twenty years ago. Seeing it, anybody would feel a bit sorry for her. There was nothing fancy about her: other than dance, she desired nothing else from this material world.

"You don't have to bring those things. Everything has been prepared," Xu Qunshan said.

With the complete faith of a child, she blankly took her old towel and bald toothbrush out again, then looked at him ingratiatingly. Everything has been prepared, she thought. Has been prepared? As expected, no one hindered them. A girl guard was downstairs, holding a huge bowl of hot noodles she had bought at the noodle stand, sweat forming on her forehead. As soon as she saw the young Commissar Xu Qunshan leading Sun Likun along, she smartly cleared a path for them. Xu Qunshan had one hand thrust in his pants pocket, the other swinging freely in a willful dignified manner. No matter how you looked at him, he was a commissar. Wielding the freely swinging hand, he pointed to a motorcycle with a sidecar parked alongside the trash dumpster and said, "Get in."

She stepped into the sidecar and sat down. He picked up his woolen overcoat off the seat and tossed it to her. The casual yet precise manner of that toss showed how his concern for her had already become second nature.

In the midst of the roar of the motorcycle's ignition, half a dozen teenage girls rushed out from inside. They all assumed that taking Sun Likun into custody like this was an official activity.

In the winter dusk, row after row of sparrows stood listlessly on the telephone wires. People walked by, disheartened. Thousands of bicycles covered with dust trudged forward on ash-covered streets and alleys. She didn't know what month, day or day of the week it was. She saw people standing in line for the public bathhouse. Three girl soldiers, eighteen or nineteen years old, were talking and laughing, their gestures made pantomime by the roar of the motorcycle. Xu Qunshan drove from the side streets onto a main street and from there onto one of the city's main concentric thoroughfares. The city looked like a badly painted chessboard. He was carrying her off, and there was no escape. He was also falling into his own trap of sweet oblivion.

In a loud voice he said to her, "It's been a long time since you've been outside!"

She understood that he was taking her on a joyride. She also understood that he was trying to decide whether to show her his final card.

Sitting below him in the sidecar, she yelled to him, "Look at that old lady selling tea eggs! Back when I was in dance school, she was already right there selling her eggs. Back then, tea eggs cost five cents apiece, and not one of them smelled bad! That candy store over there used to be a shoe repair shop! And that tailor shop didn't used to be so big!"

The darkening cityscape and the wind bored into her eyes. The wind was not at all harsh but felt as worn out as the city itself. Shreds of big-character posters hung from many of the walls, giving the whole city a tattered look.

He stopped the motorcycle in front of an old-fashioned oil-burning street lamp. At night, these street lamps constituted the city's only extravagance. Under the oil lamps, vendors with baskets and small carts would lay out unusual foodstuffs no one had ever seen during the daytime. The oil street lamps had burned for centuries. No matter during war or peace, no matter who took political center stage or who was being hooted off the stage, no matter whether Sun Likun was glorious or down on her luck, all the same they glowed there steadily, darkly illuminating those foodstuffs and the peddlers and their customers that all came from nowhere.

Stepping out of the sidecar under the oil street lamps, she happened upon several bunches of miniature bananas, as thick as pudgy fingers. It had been many years since she had seen bananas. She stood there, eyes wide open and mouth half agape as Xu Qunshan dismounted, reached into his pocket and drew out bills and coins. He made a clean sweep of the things under the street lamp. She saw him impatiently, disdainfully wait for the peddler to count through that uncountable pile of money. Each banana was equivalent to three days' worth of her meal allowance.

The bananas bore the vinegary scent of imminent rot. Yet inside they were still fragrant and sweet. He urged her to eat, and she peeled the most shapely one for him. He looked at her with a smile and stuffed the whole banana in his mouth. From his pocket he took out a square handkerchief and wiped his fingers as if they had just touched something dirty. He tossed the handkerchief to Sun Likun, the straddled his motorcycle seat. She loved every step in the series of his actions.

After they had driven ten minutes on the highway toward the outskirts of the city, he stopped the motorcycle in the courtyard of a guesthouse. She had stayed in this guesthouse before. In it were preserved certain rooms formerly occupied by leaders and great men. Some of the leaders had become enemies of the State and the People, and some of these had already died, disgraced with multiple offenses. Their rooms would then sit awkwardly empty until someone whitewashed them anew, expurgating all their awkward history.

An hour later, Sun Likun was soaking in a bathtub. It had been ages since she had taken a real bath. At most she had used a bucket of water and her face towel to wipe the grime off her body. She soaked her entire body lustrously smooth, and her heart kept floating upwards. She had already soaked to the point where she had a slight headache and felt a bit nauseous. Still, she didn't feel like stepping out of the water. She heard him out in the living room, turning the pages of the newspaper. He sat on the huge, very official-looking light blue sofa, reading the paper, occasionally clearing his throat or lifting the lid of his teacup to sip some tea. She heard a hotel employee deliver a thermos full of hot water. She basked in the sounds of his turning the pages of his newspaper and sipping tea. They created in her a kind of longing she had never felt before, a longing for being together with another person, daily and always. She knew the humbleness of this longing as well as its shattered prospects. All the pores in her body held this intuition. The only thing wanting proof was exactly *how* everything in her future would be shattered. Such circumstances as these—he in the living room reading the paper, she a wall away in the bathtub dozing off—these circumstances represented the sweetest possible living situation. She could not imagine a more satisfying emotional warmth in the world.

She stepped out of the bathtub. It had been a long time since she had stood before a mirror, and she didn't quite dare to look at her own stranger's face. Avoiding it, she put on her clothes and combed her wet hair. She had made up her mind that their last day together would be well spent.

Xu Qunshan lifted his face from the newspaper and saw how tender her overly scrubbed face looked; if you touched it, it would crack. She combed her hair for a while, waiting for his next signal.

The copper-colored bananas had been placed on the table, like precious antiques. Next to them was a gadget she didn't recognize. He said it was a portable tape player. He said he had found a tape with a selection from *The Legend of White Snake*. He turned the player on, and it emitted a seductive *erhu* solo that slowly warbled to the point of weeping. The sound quality was not good, and the music came out muffled, like real weeping.

She jutted out her chin and turned her ear toward the sound. But, just as when looking into the mirror, she didn't quite dare to listen to it. It was the solo dance in which White Snake weeps. After Xu Xian has seen Lady White turn into a snake and has died of fright, White Snake dances around and around his corpse, trying to use her body heat to warm him back to life.

"When I was little, I saw you dance this dance." Xu Qunshan lifted his gaze from the tape recorder. He sat on the edge of the sofa, one leg in front of another; this was not the usual way he placed his legs.

She thought this way of sitting rather odd, bizarre even, as if he were wearing an overly tight skirt. Unconsciously she picked the pack of cigarettes up off the tea table, then timidly put it back down again. She perceived something at once very significant and yet very strange, right on the long and black curve of his eyebrows.

Xu Qunshan patted the sofa next to him and asked if she dared come over and sit there. He was teasing her. Actually, there was not even a hint of teasing. His patting the sofa next to him in invitation was carefree, confident, nonchalant, as if saying, if you really dare, then that's your own fault. It was only her dancer's intuition that told her he was not carefree, not confident, that his movements belied effort and stiffness.

She sat down there, yet she didn't let her full weight sink down. Her two legs strongly held her submersion in check. They drew taut, revealing the shape of every muscle. He reached his hand over and stroked her hair; his fingertips carried a cool hint of cleanliness, cool as fresh green mint, that spread onto her newborn flesh, onto her long and supple neck.

Sun Likun turned her face toward him. At that instant, human and animal became equal, old and young, male and female, all absolutely equal. Soundlessly, she used the wordless language shared by human and animal alike to tell him: she was his.

Later, when she would reflect on all this, she would recall clearly that she herself undid the first button. She took off the long since passé cardigan blouse of India red, letting out the sculpted flesh of her dancer's body.

Try as she might to deny it, to refuse to see the true state of affairs, still the truth gradually took form. The truth importuned her, confronted her, so close it could be touched. In her entire life, already half a lifespan, nothing had ever presented itself in its true state. Dance *was* her life, and the vividness of her dance lay in the absence of any other reality.

Still, there was no way she could evade it. Too late: a gaffe made in plain view onstage, with no opportunity to retrieve it. That fundamental error she had intuited half-consciously now returned to confront her.

During these thirty-odd days and thirty-odd nights, every minute, every second laid a brick in an imaginary structure, yet she could not rely on it for support. The dance practice every night, the self-discipline and self-restraint—they were just building blocks in a search to be noticed. Yet she could not lean on them for support.

Xu Qunshan's cool fingertips ran over her entire body as if it were a thin shell of delicate porcelain. All the fidgeting and impatience in his fingertips were gone. Each elliptical, well-defined fingernail carefully swept over her silky skin, as if deathly afraid of snagging a thread.

She smelled the woolen military uniform's faint scent of mothballs and Great China cigarettes. The marvelous coarseness of the wool, its delicate scratchiness put her at ease again. She could continue in her intoxication against that apparently firm, stocky shoulder. Again and again, she blocked her intuition from trying to tell her a secret.

And yet everything was becoming clear. Things could not be put back as they were.

She lifted off his woolen military cap, lifting off the last mask in this spectacle. She ran her fingers through his thick black hair, so long with such beautiful waves; how nice it would be if such hair really grew above a man's face.

Xu Qunshan saw her realization. He saw the sea well up from her heart and burst forth as a tide.

Her hand came to rest on his gorgeous wavy hair. She understood everything. He knew that she understood everything. But it could not be revealed. For either of them. If it were revealed, both of them would be left with nothing. She would be left with nothing.

The dream was about to end.

The pining body of a thirty-four-year-old woman had been humiliated, toyed with, defiled by Xu Qunshan.

Tears flowed from the corners of her eyes, soaking that curly hair of Xu Qunshan's that was supposed to belong to a beautiful man.

"When I was little, I was such a fan of yours." He did everything he could not to betray his thoughts in his tone of voice or facial expression. Just play the role to its conclusion. "When I was eleven or twelve years old."

She had already heard this phrase so often she thought she would go mad. Without this phrase, would this whole farce have any major theme? Without this phrase, would this entire unintended yet meticulously knit cocoon ever have been spun? Through the mist of her tears she could see a hint of wickedness and ferocity in that boyish elegant face. She had already offered herself up. She could not give in to nausea. Before the finale, before she could pass this last day in perfection, everything had suddenly been revealed in all its paradox and sorrow.

THE OFFICIAL ACCOUNT, Part 3
A letter to the Sichuan Province Revolutionary Committee, Department of Protection

Esteemed Comrades:

After the utmost efforts of all the comrades here at the Beijing Public Security Bureau, especially the sustained struggle waged by the comrades of the Household Registration Department, all within the short interval of two months, the following has been determined:

The Xuan Wu District reports one Xu Qunshan, male, sixty-five years of age, a retired elementary school teacher. The Haidian District reports one Xu Qunshan, eight years old, male, a pupil at the No. 2 Yuquan Road Primary School, enrolled in the second grade. Dongcheng District reports one Zhao Qunshan and one Qiao Qunshan, both male and in their fifties, neither of whom has ever been outside of Beijing. Xicheng District reports one Xu Qunshan with the *shan* character for "coral" rather than the *shan* character for "mountain," who has previously come to the attention of the law enforcement authorities. Xu's father, Xu Dongsen, is one of our country's leading defense research scientists, and the type of research he is engaged in is among the nation's highest-level secrets.

In 1967 Xu Dongsen was transferred with his wife Li Rusi to a location on the Third Front and put in charge of a top-secret research project. At the end of 1968, Xu Qunshan was sent to the countryside of Shanxi Province. In 1970, Xu was sent back to Beijing because of illness. After that, Xu led an irregular existence. Xu reportedly organized a decadent underground music group that played bourgeois Western music. Xu also joined an underground book group that was ordered to disband by the Street Committee because the books they read were all of the obscene pornographic variety, such as *Anna Karenina* and *Madame Bovary*. Xu's companions included individuals who were arrested for counterfeiting an official seal and for diverting a military vehicle for private use. Because these offenses were committed by juveniles, the authorities opted for education and supervision. The offenders were placed under the oversight of the Street Committee and the Vigilance Committee of the Masses. We are currently conducting further investigations to determine whether or not Xu was directly involved in these criminal activities.

In late 1970, Xu traveled to the Xichang Region of Sichuan Province to seek out the whereabouts of the aforementioned parents engaged in scientific defense research on the Third Front. Few people have any knowledge of Xu's activity from that time onward. Based on analysis of the available information, however, we must conclude that this Xu Qunshan is unrelated to the imposter Xu Qunshan, because this particular Xu Qunshan is female.

We shall certainly increase our revolutionary vigilance and adhere firmly to the guiding words of our Great Leader Chairman Mao, "Be ever mindful of the Dictatorship of the Proletariat," as we thoroughly investigate and expeditiously strive to solve the case of the imposter "Xu Qunshan" in order to maintain the revolutionary order of our great Socialist Motherland.

With the highest revolutionary salute!

BEIJING PUBLIC SECURITY BUREAU, JUNE 1972.

THE POPULAR ACCOUNT, Part 3

They say a long time ago the middle-aged woman in Bed 160 used to be a rather famous actress and a dancer. People would make eyes at each other and say, Oh! A dancer! What's her name? Isn't it Sun? I think it is. Made a movie. Never heard of it. These days the only famous dancers are Mao Huifang and Xue Qinghua.

They say that every day before sunrise she would climb up to the platform on the rooftop and lift her feet above her head. Quite a stunt for someone her age.

They say one morning the nurse on duty bellowed out to the rooftop, "Bed 160, get down here, someone's here to see you!" That woman known as "Bed 160" came running down, and her face immediately turned white. The nurse pointed out some girl to her sitting on her bed. She was just your average young girl about twenty-something. That gal Sun isn't from around here, and she never got any visits from relatives or friends. And she never yakked with anybody in the ward. So now that somebody had come all the way to Shanghai to visit her in the hospital, she was so moved that her face turned completely white! She called the visitor "Shan-shan." The visitor called her "Elder Sister Sun." That was the way people heard them call each other from that time on.

During that first visit, Bed 160 seemed frightened by her visitor's appearance. The girl wasn't much to look at, with a short hairstyle, neither male nor female, walking around with her shoulders squared and wearing a dark blue woolen Lenin coat. Who on earth wears a Lenin coat these days? I mean, really, a Lenin coat! Aren't we living in modern times? It was made out of good material, though; it was serge, like the type they carried in the English yardage shops just after Liberation.

Later, that girl named Shan-shan came to see her every day. She would often go with her to the lawn behind the building and spread out a plastic tablecloth on the ground, setting out a picnic of canned ham and long-tailed sardines, each of them seated on a brick and eating under the sun. It's been years since we've seen anything so nice. Both of them were so friendly with each other. When they'd walk around in the courtyard, they would always have their arms around each other's waists or shoulders or else be walking hand in hand.

After that girl Shan-shan had been coming for three weeks, people began gossiping. They said when the two of them looked at each other, the light in their eyes wasn't quite right. It was like the looks exchanged between a man and a woman. Their laugh wasn't quite right either, or the sound of their speech. Once when Bed 160 was taking her afternoon nap, that gal called Shan-shan arrived and soundlessly sat down next to her bed. She kept staring at her, like she had some kind of problem, showing no shame.

They said after that the seven other women in the ward got scared and wouldn't undress in her presence.

One evening, everybody went to the hospital auditorium to see a movie. It was the ballet *The White-Haired Girl*. The first half hadn't even finished when the two of them stood up to leave, noisily banging chairs. Shan-shan's mouth was gurgling Beijing dialect: "What the hell is this here?" Her tongue, turning backward with those *r* noises, sounded barbaric yet also arrogant. They say the two of them left the auditorium hand in hand and went to that little woods next to the mortuary. They often went to those woods. That fact caught everyone's attention.

Finally someone came to a realization: maybe this Shan-shan is a man dressed up as a woman! And they both went into the woods to engage in debauchery! So the next day three nurses with six or seven robust female mental patients in tow took that Shan-shan into the women's bathroom. They say that those six or seven women, under the direction of the nurses, were only too happy to expose Bed 160's visitor—the mad betraying the mad. Some pulled open her clothes, some pulled down her pants, others pinned her as she struggled, with this result: Shan-shan was definitely, beyond any doubt, a woman.

After that, everybody completely lost interest in the two of them. No matter how intimate they were, no matter how much they would go burrow into those woods, nobody cared. What was so interesting about a couple of women?

In the winter of 1974, a black Red Flag sedan took the dancer in Bed 160 away. Much later the nurses whispered secretly among themselves that that Red Flag limousine had been sent by the premier's personal secretary. So that old vamp Sun Likun actually *had* been someone famous. If we had known earlier, we would have treated her better.

THE UNTOLD STORY, Part 6

It was that same evening. The spasms in her body became smaller and smaller. Suddenly she realized that she was still naked. She thought of running to pick up her clothes, strewn everywhere, yet at the same time she realized: since there was no opposite sex here, what was the point of concealing herself? Then the opposite realization struck her: since there was no opposite sex here, what need was there to be naked? Being naked was meaningless, worthless, insipid redundancy, just as when she went to the public baths, and among the masses of same-sex bodies, bodies exposed with total nonchalance, her own nakedness became nothingness. She racked her brains to think what the chilly touch of one person's hand on the body of another might signify when both were of the same sex. She tried hard to imagine what the results of the stroking of two identical bodies would be. There *was* no result. She looked at the face of the young person now never again to be called Xu Qunshan and spit in it.

She thought hard but found no way out of her mental quandary. Just like the mental hospital where they took her, every way out was blocked.

Xu Qunshan with the *shan* character for coral; Xu Qunshan with the *shan* character for mountain. She now had an explanation for the whole scenario from beginning to end: a girl becomes infatuated with a beautiful dancer. Isn't that perfectly understandable? Sun Likun accused the girl of playing a trick on her. She had taken advantage of her weakness, taken advantage of her plight, staged a drama that could never be concluded. One female playing such a trick was far more serious than ten males doing the same. Because she was not playing a trick; her intention was anything but that. She was sincere to the point of illness. The conventional love between the sexes Sun Likun had once understood was now sapped of all meaning, had become emptiness itself. So she spat in the young face that appeared to be the gender it was not.

She thought that was the end of it: nature which had been twisted around one way had now been twisted back again. More or less. She did not know that after a few days of deep thought she would enter into a true emptiness. Far, far off in the distance, she heard someone crying and laughing indiscriminately. She did not know that this period of indiscriminate crying and laughing would last for more than a year.

When she woke up early one morning—a year later—she discovered she had been having a dream filled with recollections. She lay on a cold, narrow steel bed looking at a broken spider web that hung from the ceiling, swaying in the air. She didn't know what to make of these real and yet unreal memories. Her entire body had become extremely sensitive, a result of all the moving and handling she had received over the past months.

She resumed her dance exercises again, arising as soon as she saw the thin sliver of dawn gradually become full and round. Then one day she heard the nurse sound her gong-and-drum-corps throat: "BED ONE-SIXTY! . . ."

It was back again, except this time it was more or less a girl. White teeth, dark and smooth skin, the hair still short and neat. Soon, when she found out that this was indeed a girl from head to toe, she began calling her "Shan-shan" with a familiarity bordering on contempt.

After Shan-shan had been stripped and publicly proclaimed a girl, the two of them had a much easier time of it. They would crowd together on one narrow bed: Shan-shan, Elder Sister Sun. Their relationship hardly struck anyone as unseemly. When Shan-shan was first called by the nickname "Shan-shan," she broke out laughing. But Sun Likun kept calling her that, and gradually she became a real Shan-shan; her atrophied docility returned to her bit by bit. No longer did she portray the young mandarin from the North; she was just Shan-shan now. Her tenderness and protectiveness were also purely those of a Shan-shan. Compared to Xu Qunshan, Shan-shan's lips were much softer, more delicate, warmer.

When they were in the woods nearby the mortuary, that year, that month, that day, she realized that she was starting to love Shan-shan. She asked Shan-shan if, when she was eleven or twelve years old . . . had she really fallen in love with her?

Shan-shan "ha-ha'd" brightly. She now rarely used words to express herself to her. Her "ha-ha" was almost as if to say: I was so silly back then. Don't consider that person as real. What you should consider as real is who you see before you.

"Back then I thought if I could just get close to you, it would be so wonderful," Shan-shan said with a self-deprecatory laugh. "Don't get angry if I tell you that until not long ago, I had forgotten you. At that time, at that age, there was so much to do! Revolutionary travels, the production brigade. Sneaking back to Beijing, then stealing books everywhere, spiriting them out through the library windows. I was a bandit for a while. I completely forgot that I was a girl."

Sun Likun looked at Shan-shan, who was speaking neither fast nor slowly.

Shan-shan said that it all really began from the day she saw her through the window. Began in earnest. She was passing through Chengdu while searching for her father, who was doing secret research on the Third Front somewhere in Sichuan Province. She had recognized her in an instant. The mad desire of her twelfth year had suddenly returned. Eventually she realized that this mad desire and all her recent actions had a mysterious connection.

Sun Likun sighed and said, "Back then I looked like a pig."

"You sure did," Shan-shan agreed.

"Did I really look like a pig?"

"It wasn't so much your person. It was your attitude, the way you carried yourself." Smiling, she comforted her. "It was you who used the word 'pig.'"

"You saw that I looked like a pig and you still came to mock me?" As she spoke, her skin became taut, as if it would snap back to a touch.

Shan-shan was about to say something, then stopped herself. She pulled out a cigarette and as she lit it, she said, "Aren't we mocking each other right now? Teasing each other, just like a man and a woman?" She spit out a puff of smoke and smiled a smile of derision toward all humanity, derision also toward herself.

"Shan-shan," Sun Likun sighed.

Shan-shan still smoked cigarettes like Xu Qunshan, her single-fold eyelids drawn down coldly. Once in a while, she would roughly brush back an occasional unruly short hair. At that moment, the former dancer truly did love Shan-shan. She loved her as the illusory Xu Qunshan, and she also loved her as the real person Shan-shan. She feared Shan-shan would disappear as Xu Qunshan had, yet she also feared that Shan-shan would forever exist in her life in this manner. Nevertheless, if she didn't love Shan-shan, whom could she love? Shan-shan was the only ray of sunshine in her life, a ray full of dust, but also full of true warmth.

One day, the Performing Arts Commission sent someone to bring Sun Likun out of the hospital. He told her she had been exonerated and now even had a new appellation: "Formerly Famous Dancer."

When Sun Likun left Shanghai for Chengdu, Shan-shan did not come with her to the train station to see her off. Now that she had resumed her normal life, should Shan-shan be part of it? Yet she knew that Shan-shan was among the crowd of people on the platform. One pair of eyes in the crowd held Shan-shan's parting tears. She wanted so much to see Xu Qunshan's tears of farewell flow through Shan-shan's eyes.

THE OFFICIAL ACCOUNT, Part 3
Chengdu Evening News—Special Report, October 15, 1980

On a recent crisp October day, we interviewed the dancer Sun Likun. It was only a week before the opening night of her solo dance performance, and Comrade Sun Likun received us wearing sweat-soaked exercise clothing. *An Evening of Solo Dance with Sun Likun,* which opens October 16 at the Jin Jiang Theater, is the first performance our province has ever staged featuring only a single individual. Comrade Sun Likun is a famous dancer of national acclaim. Although she has already entered middle age, she still practices tenaciously all the basic dance exercises, and sometimes her practice sessions can go for eight hours at a stretch, setting a splendid example for the younger generation. She is slender in body and straightforward in speech, her talk constantly punctuated by open laughter. When we brought up the nervous dysfunction from which she once had suffered, she readily told us that, thanks to the personal concern of Premier Zhou at that time, as well as the help of the leadership of the Performing Arts Troupe and her comrades, she had long since recovered her health.

Her scintillating conversation moved from her professional to her personal life. When we used the phrase "the matchmaker wears out the threshold," she said, "It's not *that* serious! Just a few friends who are a little over-eager."

Then she talked about how she had met her fiancé, though she did not reveal his name. She only said he was the foreman of an assembly shop in a factory, three years younger than she, very supportive of her dancing career and extremely considerate in her life offstage. When she would finish her exercises at noon, he would always use his lunch hour to ride his bicycle back from the outskirts of town to bring her a lunch box full of her favorite mung bean cold noodles. During the summer heat wave, he would save up the cooling summer dishes the factory allotted to him, such as iced sour plum soup and iced pudding, and use a thermos to take them to the exercise room at the theater, a fifteen-kilometer round trip, rain or shine, creating a modern love story for our times. The entire time Sun Likun talked about this man close to her heart, her face wore a smile of deep affection and revealed an inner sense of satisfaction. She heaped praise on his character, saying he was a man who valued action, not words. Although he did not quite understand her dancing, he is currently deepening his knowledge in this direction, striving to be her greatest and most loyal fan in this life.

Sun Likun said that she will get married as soon as the Performing Arts Troupe assigns her an apartment. Full of hope, she said the new apartment building's foundations have already been laid. Next spring, at the latest next summer, she will be among the first in her troupe to receive new living quarters. Having said this, her eyes revealed a happy longing, and she invited us to come be her guest in her future home.

When we parted company, we expressed our best wishes that a second springtime would bloom forth both in her dance career and in her personal life, bringing her the happiness she deserves.

THE UNTOLD STORY, Part 7

One afternoon Sun Likun, wearing a pair of black harem pants as wide as a flag, ran downstairs to take a long-distance call from Beijing.

"Shan-shan?" she asked.

On the other end came a laugh both happy and pained. "You still recognize my voice?" A pause. "I saw the review of your solo dance début. And that article. . ."

"You saw them?" she said.

"You didn't dance *White Snake!*"

"No, I didn't."

Sun Likun only heard heavy breathing on the other end but no words. "Somebody came especially to see your *White Snake*," Shan-shan finally said.

Sun Likun inhaled a breath and said, "*You* came?"

"Uh-huh."

She thought of asking Shan-shan why she hadn't come to see her backstage after the performance. But she didn't ask, because it would probably make them both uncomfortable. The two of them had never been able to shake off a faint queasiness or discomfort, even at their most intimate moments.

She thought Shan-shan must certainly have seen how her figure had faded—skin, flesh and bones no longer able to move in unified harmony. Or perhaps Shan-shan saw the people after the performance shaking hands with her perfunctorily, saying, "Over forty! Not easy, not easy!"

"When are you getting married?" Shan-shan asked.

She was a little embarrassed to answer. When she did, a white lie came out: "We can't figure out if we're going to get married or not. We don't always get along . . ." Suddenly she thought of the image of herself clumsily poking with her knitting needles during political study. She tried to be like all fiancées, knitting her man a sweater. The image of herself as such an old ungainly fiancée chagrined her, especially as she spoke to Shan-shan over three thousand kilometers away.

"How about you?" Sun Likun finally asked her.

"I'm getting married next Sunday."

"Shan-shan!. . ." she cried out.

Once again Shan-shan's manipulations had hurt her deeply.

Sun Likun hung up the phone, went back upstairs and made preparations to leave. She took a large chunk out of her savings and bought the most expensive Sichuan brocade quilt cover she could find and a jade carving. She arrived just at the conclusion of the wedding celebration. Actually, there had not been much of a wedding, just eight people getting together to drink beer and eat peanuts. No relative of Shan-shan's came to the wedding. Her parents had died during the previous year, one following the other, and her brothers and sisters lived far away.

Shan-shan was clearly no longer Xu Qunshan. Her hair was still short, her clothing still dark, and she still had that slightly sneering smile. Nevertheless, there was not a trace of Xu Qunshan left.

Sun Likun could not swallow even a single peanut. She kept looking at how Shan-shan's ten long fine fingers were still fidgeting. Fidgeting even more. She told herself that she should be happy for Shan-shan; from now on, she couldn't go *too* far wrong. She thought of her intimate but illicit connection with her, then got to thinking about how everything would now come to a halt. Shan-shan, meanwhile, was clumsily learning how to act as a woman. As she poured beer for the guests, the movements of her hands and feet were not awkward at all but full of patience and restraint. Shan-shan's husband followed her off to one side, constantly whispering encouragement to her that no one else could hear. With every move she made, his body showed a slight sympathetic movement that came from his desire to help her. He was a good man.

All the unwrapped gifts were chaotically piled up in the disorderly "nuptial chamber." It was only now, as Shan-shan took it out of the box, that Sun Likun realized the extremely intricate jade carving she had given them depicted the drama of White Snake and Blue Snake. Shan-shan looked at her as if to ask why she had dropped such an obvious hint. Sun Likun looked back at her as if to say she had not done so deliberately, that she would absolutely keep their secret to herself. Her husband was leaning his head to the left and the right, appreciating the jade carving. He thanked Sun Likun profusely, saying it was much too exquisite a gift. He was a thirty-five-year-old assistant professor, a duty-conscious man absolutely not prone to being swayed by every new idea. His appearance was not bad; his ears did not stick out in the wind and his teeth were not helter-skelter. At his side, Shan-shan would be able to gather herself together and curb all her abnormal originality. Sun Likun imagined that Shan-shan's deep appreciation for and reckless pursuit of beauty, as well as her natural empathy, could all over time be balanced and reined in by this man who was as punctilious as a textbook. Shan-shan herself understood that she had a fatal need for correction.

Shan-shan sat giggling at the end of the table facing her and with one stroke pushed away the disorderly short hair on her forehead. Sun Likun thought perhaps Shan-shan was laughing at something with the others, and started giggling as well, out of awkwardness. She laughed until she got goose bumps. Or maybe she was laughing at herself: before setting out, she had made a point of digging out that old India red cardigan blouse to wear at the wedding. Could you still call it red?

She said she had brought a small earthenware jar of rice-wine dregs, so she could make everyone a bowl of marinated hard-boiled wine eggs.

Shan-shan said, laughing: "Do you think they deserve it?"

As she was busy working over at the stove in the corridor outside the apartment, she suddenly raised her head and saw Shan-shan looking at her, a cigarette burning in her hand. Under her cold single-fold eyelids were pity and loathing. Pity and loathing were not the only emotions she was harboring. At that moment Shan-shan's husband came out carrying a stack of bowls, so that they did not have time to utter a single word.

She lied, saying that someone was waiting for her downstairs, and she could not tarry any longer. Shan-shan was looking at her, looking at her raised neck walking out the door, the neck of a wounded swan. She had left the silk scarf she had been wearing hanging on the back of her chair, and she herself was not sure whether she had left it there intentionally. Left it so that Shan-shan would have an excuse to go out in pursuit of her in the dark quiet streets. This is what Sun Likun most feared, and most desired.

As it happened, Shan-shan did call out to her on the dark quiet street. But she had not brought the silk scarf. They were like form facing its shadow, and shadow facing its form.

Why was she chasing her? To vow her to secrecy? To silence the keeper of her great secret?

"Shall I see you off?"

"Really, why go to so much trouble?"

"I'll go with you part of the way."

"Go back! You have so many guests!"

"They're his guests."

They walked together, with Shan-shan's shoulder pressed against hers. Then Shan-shan took her two or three pieces of luggage and carried them for her. When they had arrived at the first bus stop, Shan-shan said, "Let's walk to the next stop." Sun Likun had nothing to say and continued walking onward. She was still in the habit of yielding to Shan-shan.

At the third bus stop, both of them halted. Suddenly the wind came and mussed up Shan-shan's whole head of short hair. This kind of short hair was now very fashionable; they called it Zhang Yu style. Without stopping herself, Sun Likun raised her hand to put Shan-shan's hair back into place, and Shan-shan in turn stretched out her hand and wiped away a tear from one of Sun Likun's wrinkles. They both knew this was the last time they would touch each other.

As she boarded the bus, Sun Likun saw her still standing there, hands in pockets, her shoulders hunched up like a street kid's. Xu Qunshan! her heart cried out.

Notes to "White Snake"

Page 6 **Big-character posters:** posters hung in public places in China at times of political foment and used as a form of political debate to publicize opinions, essays, political treatises, denunciations, etc.

Page 6 At **struggle sessions,** a group of people would gang up on a single person to accuse and denounce him or her. They were a constant feature of the Cultural Revolution.

Page 8 **Study session:** Chinese work units generally have weekly sessions at which the workers are required to study the latest policies or documents issued by the Central Government.

Page 10 **Zongzi:** a sort of tamale with glutinous rice and other fillings (meat, raisins, sweetened bean paste, etc.) wrapped inside bamboo leaves.

Page 13 **Han:** the dominant ethnic group of China, the people most of the world refers to simply as "the Chinese," is called the Han after the Han Dynasty (206 B.C.E. – 220 C.E.). The Hui are Chinese Muslims, very close in apearance to the Han but descended from Arab, Persian and Turkic soldiers who served China's emperors. The Qiang was an ancient Caucasion tribe of Western China.

Page 13 **Cadre kids** *(gaoganzidi):* the sons and daughters of high-ranking Communist Party cadres. They often wield considerable power through their parents' influence.

Page 15 **"Wool suit":** wool was an impossibly expensive material at this time in cotton-clad China.

Page 18 **Young Pioneers:** primary school children with good marks in school and good behavior who participate in special activities and get to wear a red scarf.

Page 21 **Xu Qunshan:** pronunciation is approximately "shyh chyhn shan."

Page 28 **Wristwatch:** a proverb at the time was that a woman should only marry a man who could provide her with the "three things that go round": a wristwatch, a sewing machine and a bicycle.

Page 33 **Kang:** a type of raised platform in Northern Chinese houses that is heated. At night it serves as a bed, by day, a seating area.

Page 34 **"Mend the earth":** Maoist slogan associated with sending the educated city youth into the countryside.

Page 34 **Special soldier:** during the Cultural Revolution, young people often served in the People's Liberation Army (PLA) as "special soldiers" for certain purposes, such as the performing arts.

Page 34 **Intellectual Youth:** city youth who had made it past middle school. They were sent to the countryside to teach the peasants and to learn from them.

Page 46 **Erhu:** a two-stringed violinlike instrument played with a bow, typically used in Chinese classical music and Chinese opera.

Page 51 **Famous dancers:** during this period, culture was under the sway of Mao's wife Jiang Qing who permitted only a small number of "model revolutionary operas," such as *The White-Haired Girl*, to be performed. Only a small number of ballet dancers who enjoyed her official favor were allowed to perform in them.

Page 51 **Shan-shan:** typical nickname for a girl with the "shan" character for coral as part of her given name. *Sun Jie*, literally "Elder Sister Sun," would be a normal and proper way for a younger woman to address Sun Likun.

Page 51 **Liberation:** the takeover of mainland China by the Communists in 1949.

Page 57 **Open laughter:** East Asian tradition discourages women from laughing or even showing their teeth.

Page 61 **"Egg"** is a common way in Chinese to refer to a despicable person.

Page 61 **Her great secret:** lesbian activity is illegal in China and can result in official punishment as well as social ostracism.

天浴 Celestial Bath

TRANSLATOR'S NOTE: *This story is set in the grasslands of China's Sichuan Province at the border of Tibet in the mid-1970s, during the waning years of the Cultural Revolution, when many young people from the cities who had been sent to the countryside to do various types of labor and "learn from the masses" started to make their way back to the cities. The teenaged girl in this story is learning how to raise horses for the army, even though—unbeknownst to her—its cavalry units have long since been disbanded.*

The clouds brushed over the sharp blades of grass. The shafts, heavy with seed, undulated, each wave bowing before the next.

Wen Xiu sat on the slope watching Lao Jin run downhill, becoming small as a prairie dog. Wen Xiu had been chosen by Lao Jin from among the Intellectual Youth to learn how to herd horses. The day she had followed Lao Jin to the herding site, she saw there was only one yurt-like, round military tent and realized she would have to share it with Lao Jin. Before she had come out, the Livestock Bureau had told Wen Xiu that there was no need for concern about Lao Jin: his thing had been lopped off long ago. Some decades before, there had been a blood feud out here. The opposing clan had grabbed Lao Jin, then eighteen years old, and run a knife between his legs. Since then he had been bereft of his manhood. There had already been six, maybe seven, girls among the Intellectual Youth who had learned how to herd horses with him, and none had ever come back carrying Lao Jin's foal. The feuding war party had definitely scraped him clean.

Nonetheless, Wen Xiu detested Lao Jin. If it weren't for Lao Jin's choosing her, she would still be together with several hundred other Intellectual Youth back at the powdered milk plant. One time she asked Lao Jin why it was he had selected her, of all people, to herd horses. Lao Jin replied, "You have a horse's face."

Wen Xiu was not considered ugly; back in middle school in Chengdu, she certainly wasn't. She was just a little short and skinny. Her body was like a wasp's, her waist only two hand clasps in circumference, making it look like she had two segments. When she mounted or dismounted a horse, Lao Jin would run up to her with both hands taut and outstretched and say, "Up we go!" or "Down we go!" He would hold her, supporting her buttocks with one hand and using the other to lift her by the underarm. Wen Xiu sensed that Lao Jin's hands really wanted to do something else. She hadn't been on the prairie for long before several men tried to feel her up, and it was usually done under the guise of teaching her how to mount or dismount a horse. Afterward, Wen Xiu herself would surreptitiously touch the parts that the men had touched, as if by doing so she could restore them. The Livestock Bureau put on outdoor movies. When the movie was over, as soon as the generator was shut off, ten or more Intellectual Youth girls would yelp, "Bastard! Damn your ancestors!" They had all been felt up. At that moment several dozen flashlights would intersect their beams, their shafts of light piercing the night sky like spears planted helter-skelter. That was just how the guys here got their jollies.

Since she had started herding with Lao Jin, she had not been to see a movie. In order to go, she would have had to sit behind Lao Jin on a horse, hanging on to his waist for twenty or thirty kilometers. The last thing Wen Xiu wanted to do was to hug Lao Jin's waist, and if that meant no movies, then so be it.

Around ten kilometers from the tent, at the foot of a slope, there was a shallow stream. The only way Lao Jin could collect water was by dragging a leather pouch flat along the stream's bottom. Yet any time that Wen Xiu complained of itchiness, Lao Jin would tell her there was a way to take a bath. She would hear him singing as he drew water and knew that he was singing for her ears only. Lao Jin was a first-rate singer. His singing had the music on the loudspeakers of the Livestock Bureau beat hands down! Sometimes his song sounded like a horse whinnying, other times like a sheep laughing. When she heard it, Wen Xiu felt like tumbling down the grassy slope, even though Lao Jin seemed to be singing about his troubled heart and his inexpressible dreams.

Lao Jin was singing his way back from the stream. His singing came closer. As he climbed up the grassy slope, she could already smell the horse scent on his body.

He smiled at her. His beard was withered, and his chin was barren. Sometimes, when he was idle, he would fumble with the remnants, seeking out dead bristle, then rooting it out.

She looked at him with one eye shut to avoid the bright sunlight. "Hey, Lao Jin! Why'd you stop singing?"

"Got work to do."

"But you sing so well!" It was the truth. There were times when she hated him. Hated herding horses with him. Hated sharing a tent with him. At times she wished Lao Jin would just die — but not the song. The song should follow her, even when she left this place.

"Gotta stop singing," Lao Jin said, smiling bashfully.

Wen Xiu hated his gold front tooth, which ruined a perfectly good smile. If it weren't for that, he would not have looked nearly so fierce and frightening.

Lao Jin's full name was Jin something-something, four syllables long. If you were walking behind a band of Tibetans and called out that name, at least ten of them would turn around in response. Wen Xiu didn't bother to remember the name. Lao Jin, Lao Jin—much easier for everybody. Lao Jin was forty-something years old, but he looked older than that. Tibetans don't keep track of their birthdays, so you couldn't be sure if he was still in his thirties or had already reached fifty. Unlike other old herdsmen in the Livestock Bureau, Lao

Jin had not accumulated any personal property. He owned neither a wristwatch nor a fountain pen. His most valuable possession was his gold tooth, and even this he had inherited from his mother. She had told Lao Jin to knock it out as soon as she died, so the man who performed the sky burial couldn't take it. He later had the knifesmith inlay his own tooth with the gold. The knifesmith knew how to inlay any bone-handled knife, and he used the same technique to inlay Lao Jin's tooth.

The water-filled leather saddlebags dangled on both sides of the horse's rump. Lao Jin lightly whipped the horse's round buttocks with his palm, and the horse hauled the water up the slope. The horse's belly, stuffed pendulously round from grazing, crooked off to the left, then to the right. Lao Jin followed its gait, his stocky muscular shoulders dipping and angling down this way, then that way.

If you didn't know his story, you couldn't tell that Lao Jin lacked anything that other men had. Especially when Lao Jin lassoed a horse. His whole body formed one unbroken arc with the rope, taut as a bowstring. Once the horse straightened its legs to run, Lao Jin had him. In these prairies there wasn't another man for hundreds of miles around who had such a deft and powerful hand.

Lao Jin poured the two big leather saddlebags full of water into the oblong ditch he had dug at the summit of the slope. The ditch was rather shallow. A little deeper and one could just fit a coffin in it. The ditch was lined with a sheet of black plastic from a torn-up bag of horse fodder.

Wen Xiu sat downhill from the ditch, her body facing down the slope, her head turned back toward Lao Jin. After watching him for a while, she asked, "What are you doing?"

"You'll see," Lao Jin replied.

He peeled off his shirt. It had been soaked with sweat and dried by the sun, so it was pasted to his back like a medicinal compress. When it came off, it made a "ssslah!" sound, and a puff of vapor blew out. As he poured out the contents of the saddlebags, the water in the little pool rose. It was over half full.

Wen Xiu's neck was sore from turning her head back to look.

"What are you up to now?" she persisted.

"Just wait and see," Lao Jin replied in a low growl. Every time Wen Xiu got on or off a horse and didn't want Lao Jin to help her, his lips would part over that gold tooth while he growled like that. The sound contained a womanly pique completely inconsistent with Lao Jin's massive trunk and wide prairie face. There was also a sort of beastlike affection in it.

Wen Xiu stared blankly down the slope toward the horses. Lao Jin took a seat on the ground not far from her, pulled out a tobacco pouch, rubbed the tobacco leaves on his thigh and rolled himself a fat thick cheroot. Then he stuck it in his mouth and began lighting it all the way around. Wen Xiu heard the crude matches skittering, heard them breaking, and looked at Lao Jin as he fumbled with his makeshift cheroot, giving him a narrow-eyed smirk of "serves you right." Only after ten or so matches had been broken or extinguished in the wind did he succeed in lighting the cheroot, which protruded sideways out his mouth like some kind of artillery cannon. Under the bright noonday sun, you couldn't see the lit end of the cheroot and you couldn't see the smoke, just stringlike shadows swirling about Lao Jin's face. The smoke stank: as the cheroot burned shorter, the stench grew worse.

Smoke was also rising off the little pool. Inside its vapor, the transparent air warped and shimmered. The sunlight was absorbed by the black plastic, heating the water. And all in less time than it took Lao Jin to enjoy his cheroot.

Curious, Wen Xiu walked up the slope toward the pool at the summit. She tested the water with her hand and cried out, "It's scalding hot!"

"You can bathe in it now," Lao Jin replied.

"How about you?"

"Go ahead, you bathe. Pretty soon it will be too hot to bear."

She knew Lao Jin didn't bathe. The first time he had held Wen Xiu dismounting from a horse, she realized that this was a man who had never taken a bath in his life.

"I'm going to take my clothes off now," Wen Xiu said.

"Go ahead," Lao Jin replied, continuing to stare.

Wen Xiu pointed down the slope toward the herd. "You go round up the horses. Some of them look like they're about to stampede."

Lao Jin, a little put out, slowly turned his head away from her. "I'm not going to watch you."

Wen Xiu squatted on the ground. "But I can't bathe with you here!"

Lao Jin didn't move. He knew she wouldn't pass up the chance of bathing. She loved to bathe. The first night she'd ladled out a basin of water and put it at the foot of her straw bedroll and blown out the lamp. Just as she had stripped off her panties, she heard the rustling sound of Lao Jin's straw bedroll stirring.

As she had squatted, straddling the basin of water, carefully dipping the towel in the water so as not to make a sound, Lao Jin had become deathly quiet. She felt as if Lao Jin's ear hairs were standing on end.

"Bathing?" Lao Jin had finally said in an intimate tone.

She had paid no attention to him but splashed temperamentally with her hands, making the water sound like a flock of ducks landing on a pond.

Lao Jin had then taken the initiative to break the embarrassing silence, saying, "Heh, heh! You Chengdu girls just can't get along without bathing."

It was from that time that her hatred for Lao Jin had begun. The next day she had slapped together a canvas partition to wall off the corner with her cot and bedroll from the rest of the tent.

By now, Wen Xiu was almost completely undressed. "You mustn't turn your head," she warned.

Lao Jin had his back toward Wen Xiu. He raised his head to look at the sky and remarked, "The clouds are coming this way."

Wen Xiu, now completely naked, said, "You're not allowed to turn your head!"

Then she stepped into the pool. First she let the hot water roll over her and hissed with relief as she soaked in it. It made her feel so good that she gave out a silly giggle. She knelt in the pool and used the hand-sized washcloth to scoop up water onto her body.

Lao Jin sat rigidly immobile without turning his head. The place where he sat was lower down on the slope. If he turned his head, he could not see Wen Xiu completely. Wen Xiu, however, kept staring vigilantly at the back of his neck while she rubbed her body with scented soap. Before she picked up the soap, she first shook her hand dry. If her hands were too wet, it would waste soap. That's what her mother had taught her. Wen Xiu's father was a tailor and knew how to save customers' cloth. In all the years her parents had been married, Wen Xiu's mother had never had to buy her own cloth.

"Lao Jin, sing another song!" Wen Xiu requested, now finished with washing and enjoying a good soak.

"The clouds are moving this way." Lao Jin shifted his gaze from one end of the sky to the other, as if watching the clouds move, then deliberately turned his head toward where Wen Xiu was. He saw her flour white shoulders with a dark-burnt face perched on top. The whiteness of her body in the pool appeared a blur, like moonlight stroked and ruffled on troubled waters.

Wen Xiu cried out shrilly, "Damn you, Lao Jin!" and she splashed soapy water at him.

Lao Jin quickly turned his face back around, sat down again properly and wiped the water off his face with his green cotton Mao cap.

"May your eyes rot out!" Wen Xiu cursed.

"I didn't see anything," Lao Jin protested, still wiping water off the tip of his nose and lips.

"If you did see anything, may your eyes rot out!"

"I saw nothing."

After a while Wen Xiu was ready to get dressed again. At the bottom of the slope, two men came by, each astride a yak. They were driving a herd of yaks to the slaughterhouse. Both of them were quite familiar with Lao Jin and called out, "Lao Jin! Lao Jin! What are you doing squatting up there?"

"Don't come up!" Lao Jin growled back.

"What are you doing? Squatting to take a piss, huh?" Having said this, the man at the front yanked the reins of the yak he was riding and circled around the back of the slope, heading for the summit.

"Don't come up!" Lao Jin quickly turned his head toward Wen Xiu and barked, "Get dressed."

By now the men had discovered Wen Xiu cowering there, covering up her body, but they still pretended they had come up to give Lao Jin a hard time. "Lao Jin, everyone says you've got to squat like a woman to take a piss. Today we caught you in the act. We want to watch!"

Lao Jin dragged his rifle off the ground and looked through the sights, carefully sizing up the two of them. When the pair tried to proceed forward, the rifle sounded. One of the yaks reared up into the air, then turned its head and careened down the slope diagonally, its body in profile. It was now shorn of one horn and had lost all sense of balance and direction.

The man who had been bucked off the yak, called, "How dare you shoot at us, Lao Jin, you son of a bitch!"

Lao Jin dribbled some spittle onto the rifle barrel and wiped off the gunpowder stain with the corner of his jacket. He made no sound and showed no expression, but just acted as if nothing had happened. Then he loaded another bullet into the rifle's belly and said to the other man, who was still sitting dumbfounded on his yak not knowing whether to advance or retreat, "You want one, too?"

The man hastily pulled the yak's head around. From its back he yelled, "Just you wait, Lao Jin, you son of a bitch!"

"Wait for what? For you to come and bite my balls? I ain't even got my tool no more!" Lao Jin yelled. With both hands he slapped his crotch, whacking it powerfully, pounding a fair amount of dust out of his trousers.

Wen Xiu burst out laughing. She felt Lao Jin's fearlessness was genuine: without that thing to determine his fate, no one could threaten his life.

By a certain evening in October, Wen Xiu had been herding horses with Lao Jin for exactly half a year. That is to say, she had graduated. She could now lead a platoon of Intellectual Youth girls in herding horses. In the morning she woke up early, stuck her head out from behind her canvas partition and asked Lao Jin, "Do you think they'll come today to take me back to the Livestock Bureau?"

Lao Jin had just entered the tent, cradling in the crook of his arm a load of firewood wrapped in a layer of white frost. "Huh?" he replied.

"It's been six months already. They said after six months I could return to the Livestock Bureau. It's been one hundred and eighty days. I've counted them."

Lao Jin relaxed his grip, and the firewood came rolling out onto the ground. He was wearing a military fur coat with his own alterations. Both the sleeves had been removed, exposing his long apelike arms from the shoulder, which gave him the appearance of being both dexterous and clumsy. He was looking at Wen Xiu.

"You're leaving?"

"Leaving?" she replied. "It's my turn to leave." She gaily tilted her sharp little chin as she drew her head back behind the canvas curtain.

She started laying out clothes, deciding what to wear. From two identical old outfits she pulled out one, held it up to the light and looked at how many tiny holes had been shot through it by sparks from the fire pit. No, that wouldn't do. She looked at the other outfit, but it wasn't much better. With a sigh, she finally put it on. With a gauze scarf and her hair combed nicely, she wouldn't look too messy. When she stepped out of her enclosure, Lao Jin had already brought the butter tea to a noisy boil.

Making conversation, Wen Xiu asked, "Have you eaten yet?"

"Cooking," Lao Jin replied, pointing to the fire.

Seeing her nicely dressed and made up, his eyes followed her, his hands mechanically snapping off twigs. Then she took a piece of mirror broken in a triangular shape and handed it to him. Immediately he stood up and held it for her. She didn't need to say a word.

He would raise and lower it according to her unspoken wishes.

Wen Xiu spent a week in this manner, arranging her gauze scarf and braiding her hair. The person who should have come from the Livestock Bureau to take her back had not come. On the eighth day, Lao Jin said, "We've got to break camp and move on from here. The heavy rains have changed the course of the stream. There won't be any water for the horses to drink, and there won't be any for us either."

Immediately Wen Xiu started to protest loudly. "*Move* again? Move *again?* When the Livestock Bureau sends someone for me, we'll be even harder to find." She glared at Lao Jin, her small round eyes quivering out two accusatory teardrops—the Livestock Bureau must've all died off, seven days without seeing hide or hair of them, and all of this is your fault, Lao Jin!

As the days passed, Lao Jin did not bring up the matter of moving camp any more. Every day he took the horses farther afield to find grass that was not too parched. Wen Xiu no longer herded horses with him. She spent each day waiting at the entrance of the tent.

One day someone arrived. It was a peddler with an ox cart selling goods to all the various herding camps. He asked Wen Xiu if he could come in for some buttered tea. As they sat on the floor and talked, he told Wen Xiu that over the past half year, the Intellectual Youth had begun to be withdrawn from the herding camps and were returning to the city. The first to go were those whose families had clout. Next were those with good connections at the Livestock Bureau. Almost all the girls among the Intellectual Youth had gone: they had all established a "good connection" to the Livestock Bureau.

When Wen Xiu heard this, she stood there with her mouth gaping.

"Why haven't you left?" the peddler asked, as if prying at some shameful secret of hers.

"They've all gone, and I'll go, too . . . when I feel like it . . . go back to Chengdu." Both the peddler's knees pressed against Wen Xiu's knees.

Wen Xiu stared at him blankly. The peddler was apparently a former soldier. He had a pair of eyes that had seen it all. All the good jobs out here went to ex-soldiers.

"For a girl like you," the peddler said, "getting good connections at the Livestock Bureau should be no problem at all!" He laughed and spoke no more. Then his lips went to Wen Xiu's face, neck, between her breasts . . .

The peddler lay on top of Wen Xiu groping and rolling, crushing the straw in the bedroll. Wen Xiu wanted to go back to Chengdu. Her mother and father couldn't help her. She could only rely on herself to find a way out. The peddler was the first way out that she found.

As the day was approaching evening and Lao Jin walked back into the tent, he heard the rustling of straw behind Wen Xiu's canvas curtain. Under the curtain, Lao Jin could see a pair of men's cloth shoes tossed on the ground, soles facing upward. Lao Jin didn't realize that he had been standing in the tent, immobile, for over an hour, until everything was pitch black both inside and outside the tent.

The peddler came out from behind the canvas partition wearing the cloth shoes, the backs crushed flat. He didn't see Lao Jin. The peddler went straight to the opening of the tent, lit up by the rising moon. The ox harnessed to the cart woke from its slumber as the peddler climbed in. He turned on a transistor radio and rode off, singing as he went.

From Wen Xiu's bed came not a hint of human sound. She was still alive; she just lay there as if dead, turning her eyeballs back and forth awkwardly in the darkness. "Lao Jin? Lao Jin, is that you?"

"Uhn," Lao Jin grunted in reply, shuffling his footsteps around to signify that everything was normal.

"Lao Jin, is there any water?"

Lao Jin brought over a cup of butter tea. Wen Xiu's head popped out from under the canvas curtain. Just then, the moonlight shone on it, and Lao Jin saw that her head and face were soaked with sweat, wet like a newborn lamb. She drew her mouth closer to drink. Lao Jin leaned forward and supported her head. She frowned slightly, as if to extricate herself from the palm of Lao Jin's hand.

"No water, huh?" she said in an accusatory tone.

"Uhn," Lao Jin grunted once more and dashed out of the tent. He dragged over his riding horse. Swinging his leg over its back, he gave it a vicious kick with his heels.

Lao Jin rode the ten kilometers to the little brook at the foot of the hill, the one where he had drawn water for Wen Xiu to bathe in that day under the hot sun. He took two military canteens and filled them until they could hold no more. By the time he got back, the moon was already high in the sky. Wen Xiu was still inside her canvas enclosure in the corner of the tent.

"Come have a drink! Water's here!" Lao Jin called out, almost gaily.

He passed a canteen through to Wen Xiu. Very soon he heard an "oo-too! oo-too! oo-too!" sound as she poured it into the metal basin. After a while, Wen Xiu stuck her hand out again, beckoning for the second canteen.

"I brought it for you to drink," Lao Jin protested.

Saying nothing, she just snatched the strap of the canteen and dragged it inside her canvas enclosure. Once again he heard the sound of water. She was bathing again. She just couldn't get along without bathing, Lao Jin thought—especially today. After a while, she threw some clothes on and walked out, carrying the basin of water with both hands. She walked out of the tent and went a considerable distance before she finally threw out the water.

To Lao Jin, the way she walked was no longer very becoming.

"Lao Jin," she said, handing him one of the canteens deferentially, "there's still a little water left. Would you like a drink?"

"You drink it," Lao Jin replied.

Insisting no more, she took an apple out of her pocket and carefully aimed the spout of the canteen at it. The water came out in a thin stream. She turned the apple evenly with her other hand, washing it on all sides. She raised her eyes and saw that Lao Jin was looking at her. She smiled briefly and then began, "ka-chaw, ka-chaw!" to gnaw on the apple. The peddler had given it to her. She held it with both hands while she gnawed on it. There was really no need to use both hands, however: it was quite small.

Wen Xiu continued to stay in the tent all day while Lao Jin went out to herd horses. Every night when Lao Jin returned, he would see a big pair of men's shoes under the canvas curtain. One time a shoe had been tossed a couple of meters outside the curtain, almost to the edge of the fire pit in the middle of the tent. Lao Jin picked up the fire tongs in one hand. He looked at the shoe as it lay there, sizing it up. Then he grasped the shoe with the fire tongs and dropped it into the fire. The shoe's leather roasted until it sizzled and small beads of oil began to seep out. Then it started to twist and puff out cloying clouds of smoke which gradually turned to ashen white. Its stench filled the whole tent.

Lao Jin recognized this shoe. Few people in the grasslands could afford to strut about in a shoe like this. There was one pair in the Communist Party Committee of the Livestock Bureau, two in the Livestock Bureau's Personnel Department. Only these three.

A few days before, Wen Xiu had told Lao Jin, "These people coming to see me are important people, you know."

"How important?" Lao Jin had asked.

"Extremely important. They all have the power to approve documents. To go back to Chengdu, without some important people to approve some documents and stamp their seals on them, there is no way out." She looked at Lao Jin, but it was hard to say where her gaze was focused. Her tone of voice was a low monotone, just as when Lao Jin was bored and frustrated and went outside to pour out his heart quietly to his horses.

For his part, Lao Jin looked at her with a dazed expression, like an animal that understands emotions but doesn't understand human language. She hadn't been out herding for some days now, and a layer of skin on her face, scorched by the intense sun, had started to peel off. Through the cracks of the burnt surface, pinkish tender flesh had begun to appear. While she was talking, her nails would fly quickly over the skin on her face, scraping lightly. Her sharp fine nails gradually picked open a fissure; then a spot of new flesh about the size of a wild broadbean flower began to emerge.

"I'm too late—all the other Intellectual Youth girls did this years ago to get the Livestock Bureau to send them home. By now they've probably all found jobs in Chengdu. Think of it, a girl with no money and no connections, isn't this the only asset she's got left?" As she spoke, she lifted up her eyes, as if to express her justification. She also told him it wouldn't work if she slept with one without sleeping with the others. Those you didn't sleep with would block your way.

Lao Jin nodded his head as he rolled a stronger than usual cheroot on his thigh. Wen Xiu had told him everything. She didn't tell him because she particularly cared about his opinion. Just the opposite—it was because he couldn't possibly have an opinion. After all, what kind of opinions could livestock have?

The canvas curtain rustled for a bit. The man was looking for his second shoe. He kept groaning "son of a bitch." Lao Jin sat with his spine turned toward the curtain, smoking his cheroot, puffing vigorously, flattening out his lungs.

The man was in a tight spot. He couldn't allow Lao Jin to see him under the kerosene lamp and make a one hundred percent positive identification. He was much too important a person in the Livestock Bureau for that, and terribly busy. When he had arrived, he hadn't even bothered to exchange a polite greeting with Wen Xiu; he just went straight to what he had come for. Since her lamp had been dark the whole time, he didn't have any idea what Wen Xiu looked like.

The man's predicament caused Wen Xiu to confront Lao Jin. "Lao Jin, did you see a leather shoe anywhere?"

"Whose shoe?" Lao Jin answered.

"What do you care? Did you see it?" Wen Xiu said, raising her voice. She walked over to stand directly in front of him. Her hair hung disheveled on both sides of her face. Her body was enveloped in a green military overcoat, revealing a slice of breast at the top, a shaft of thigh at the bottom. The light from the fire pit danced on her face, which had become so thin that it looked hollow, and her sunken eye sockets looked like a pair of caves.

"I *asked* you a *question!*" she said even louder, both pleading and demanding.

Lao Jin only paid attention to his smoking, inhaling until his chest cavity was taut, then flattening it out like a bellows.

"What are you, a yak? Don't you understand people-talk. . .?" Wen Xiu huffed as she squatted down on the ground in front of him, the bottom of the overcoat parting, revealing both that which may be exposed and that which may not be. It was as if in front of livestock there was nothing to be ashamed of, as if human modesty were superfluous.

Lao Jin heard the important person slip out behind his back, half-shod.

Wen Xiu was still wrapped in her overcoat, pacing back and forth bare-legged through the tent. She picked up a canteen and rattled it. Empty. The other one, also empty. They had been camped out on this bone-dry stretch for over a month now. Every day Lao Jin had had to ride the ten kilometers to fetch two canteens of water. From that day on, her water supply was cut off.

For five days there was no water. To drink, there was only milk and buttered tea. No longer did just one man a day come to see Wen Xiu; sometimes there were two, even three. At night, no sooner would Lao Jin hear one leave than the next would come in practically on his heels. The path to the door of the tent had been trodden smooth. Lao Jin hung a piece of dry thornbush in the doorway, hoping to scratch somebody's eyes out with it. But they all stealthily tiptoed around it. Now, the most important precaution they took before climbing into Wen Xiu's bed was carefully to hide their shoes.

At dawn of the fifth day, Wen Xiu was practically at her wits' end. She hadn't slept all night and couldn't figure out who the men were that she had been with. After the very last one had left, she finally crawled out of bed. Lao Jin watched from his own bed as she dragged her footsteps over toward his bedroll and declared to him, "Lao Jin, for days there hasn't been a single drop of water!"

Lao Jin looked into her two wild eyes and saw that they were bloodshot. He also got wind of a not-to-be-reasoned-with type of odor emanating from her body. With the loss of her water supply, she seemed to have lost her last shred of dignity and rationality.

Lao Jin slowly, in a stately manner, started putting on his clothes, muttering as he dressed. His pants, spotted with sweat stains and permeated with dust, had become so stiff that they almost stood up by themselves at his bedside. He pulled them over and began to put them on, though it wasn't clear whether he was wearing them or they were wearing him.

Wen Xiu walked over to the extinguished fire pit, her eyes scrutinizing the strip of twisted and burnt shoe sole, not registering what it was. She yelled at Lao Jin at the top of her voice, "What the hell are you doing, dressing so slow?"

Lao Jin immediately stopped his movements.

Wen Xiu, sensing something less than wonderful on its way, mouthed an even worse rebuke and glared at him.

Lao Jin walked up to her. "You're prostituting yourself, don't you know?"

Wen Xiu was still glaring at him. Then she gave him a sidelong glance and a coquettish little sneer. "What did you say?"

"You're a whore," he said.

"Not for you," she answered.

By *Li Dong*, the Beginning of Winter, Wen Xiu lay in the infirmary. She had just had an abortion. Her bare legs lay on a two-inch-thick sheet of grainy brown blotting paper to absorb the flow of blood. Lao Jin kept a vigil outside her room, waiting for someone to call him in. But no one ever did. The nurses all openly referred to Wen Xiu as "Worn-out Shoe" and "the wild nymphet." It was just

like that Intellectual Youth boy in the surgery ward whom people
openly referred to as "Zhang Three-Toes." Supposedly his rifle had
misfired and shot off three of his toes. After his wounds had healed,
Zhang Three-Toes was headed back to Chengdu. He was trading all
his possessions for caterpillar grass. Once he got to Chengdu, it
would fetch a good price at any reputable herbal medicine shop, and
besides, it was light to carry. Everybody knew that he had purpose-
fully taken aim at his foot and sheared off his toes, crippling himself.
Once he could no longer ride a horse, all they could do was send him
back to Chengdu.

On the third day of Lao Jin's vigil for Wen Xiu, Zhang Three-Toes
walked by and sat next to him on the same bench. He gave Lao Jin a
cigarette, then entered Wen Xiu's hospital room.

It was only after he had smoked the cigarette halfway down that
Lao Jin felt something was wrong. Suddenly he stood up and pushed
on the door of the room. It was locked from the inside. Lao Jin
extended his legs and took a stance, then sent his bronze-tipped
boots flying and flashing against the door. His roars of "You animal!
You beast!" caused the whole shift of nurses to come running. Soon
all the beds in the ward were empty as well. Even the paraplegic
patients rolled their wheelchairs down the hall to gawk at the commotion at Wen Xiu's door.

Several nurses restrained Lao Jin from kicking the door, but he
kept yelling "Beast! Beast!" His cries grew progressively hoarser.

Zhang Three-Toes walked out of Wen Xiu's door, and everyone
cleared a path for him. He tossed back his greasy head of hair with
the devil-may-care attitude of a proud hoodlum. Addressing the
crowd, he said, "What are you doing? What's the fuss? If you want
in, get in line!" He pointed at Wen Xiu's door, then pointed at Lao
Jin. "Lao Jin's first in line, I'll vouch for that!"

Lao Jin lifted up one of his bronze-tipped boots and stamped it
down on Zhang Three-Toes's remaining toes. Zhang Three-Toes
neighed like a horse.

The nurses yelled at the crowd to disperse. Then they had a loud
discussion among themselves.

"It wouldn't matter to her if it were a stud donkey!"

"The bleeding just stopped and already she's luring guys into her bed."

Lao Jin returned to his place on the wooden bench.

In the middle of the night, a blizzard started. Lao Jin was awakened by the cold. He saw that Wen Xiu's door was open, but her bed was empty. He waited a while; she did not return. Lao Jin went outside to search for her, shivering with panic. He found her at the side of the road, fallen to the ground. The snow had coated her hair white. She said she had gone out to get some water. She really missed water; she wanted to take a nice, refreshing bath.

Lao Jin picked her up and embraced her, her body flush against his own. Her face was swollen to the point of transparency, but it was still pretty. Her little wasplike body was pitifully small, shivering and trembling inside the palms of Lao Jin's enormous hands. Lao Jin held Wen Xiu for a while, standing in the blizzard. He did not take her back to the infirmary. He carried her toward the stables where his horse was kept. Each time the wind came up, he would turn his spine toward it, walking backward. Wen Xiu drifted in and out of consciousness. At one point, she felt something warm dropping on her face, and she was astonished. She never thought that he might be able to cry, or that he would shed tears for her.

The next day, the sky had cleared. The grass on the prairie was covered in mournful white. The scrub was bereft of its leaves; on its tightly interlaced twigs hung bright crystalline icicles.

Lao Jin was sitting under a scrub tree, watching Wen Xiu a short distance away fumbling with the rifle. She had already told him that today was the day she wanted to carry out her plan. She had learned something from Zhang Three-Toes. Lao Jin's cheroot dangled from his mouth, long since extinguished. He waited for the rifle to sound.

The shadow of Wen Xiu's ravaged body was delicate and small, and one of her braids had come undone. For some reason, she turned her head to look at him.

He said nothing and showed no expression; the extinguished cannonlike cheroot between his lips made no motion.

She smiled at him briefly. Then she placed the rifle on the ground. "I'm afraid I won't aim right," she said. "It's hard to shoot yourself. I just can't bear to do it." Her voice was quavering.

She smiled again and put the mouth of the rifle on her foot, raised her chin and closed her eyes, like a child not daring to face its pain. "That's better. Hey, just as soon as I fall over, you'll take me right to the clinic, won't you?"

"I will," Lao Jin replied.

"I'm going to shoot now—hey, you'll tell them that I was carrying my rifle and it accidentally went off, won't you?"

"Of course I will," Lao Jin replied again.

Her face was white as snow, her lips chewed blue. The rifle still did not sound. She spoke to Lao Jin again. "Lao Jin, turn your head away. Don't look at me."

Lao Jin pulled his green Mao cap straight down to his chin, confining his face inside it. For a while, outside his hat, it was eerily quiet. He lifted his hat to take a look and saw her on the snowy ground, rolled up into a little ball, the rifle lying on the ground one pace away.

Her face full of tears, she said to Lao Jin, "Lao Jin, I beg you, please help me. I just can't bear to shoot myself..."

Lao Jin looked at her.

"Lao Jin, I'm begging you, if you get one good shot off, I can go back to Chengdu. Winter's coming. There's nothing I hate more than the winters here! None of them would help me. You help me, please! You're the only one who can help me now...!" Suddenly she rushed over, hugged Lao Jin tightly and pressed her mouth against his lips, dry and acrid with years of accumulated tobacco smoke.

Lao Jin extricated himself from her embrace and went to pick up the rifle. She gazed at him like one who is rescued, with a look of complete trust.

Lao Jin held the rifle across his body and retreated a few paces. Then he retreated a few more.

Wen Xiu stood up straight, looking directly toward the rifle barrel.

Suddenly, she asked Lao Jin to wait. She carefully plaited the braid which had come undone. Her eyes kept looking at Lao Jin. She smiled again wanly.

Instantly he understood. From her poise and her unperturbed manner, he understood the detachment, the transcendence of a farewell. He suddenly knew what she wanted him to do.

Lao Jin set the rifle to his shoulder. Gradually he raised the rifle barrel higher. She remained motionless, as if about to have her picture taken.

The rifle sounded. Wen Xiu swooned and fluttered to the ground, her mouth emitting the groan of a woman at her moment of peak satisfaction. Lao Jin put down the rifle; he knew there would be no need for a second shot.

When the sun had reached the middle of the sky, Lao Jin placed Wen Xiu's pure, pure white body into the shallow rectangular pool. It had been filled with snowy slush which Lao Jin had now heated to the temperature that had always made her feel most comfortable.

Her eyes were closed, and in the vapor her body looked like the image of an Immortal on a temple fresco.

Lao Jin now removed his own clothes. He studied carefully his own body's incompleteness, then looked at the peaceful Wen Xiu. He turned the rifle barrel around, aiming it at his own breast. One end of a rope was tied to the trigger, the other end to a stone. Then he kicked the stone, and as the stone rolled down the slope, a shot rang out, and hot blood gushed out of his chest.

Lao Jin crawled toward Wen Xiu and submerged himself in the pool. He held Wen Xiu. In a little while, the snow would cover them both completely.

Notes to "Celestial Bath"

Page 65 **Wen Xiu**: pronounced "wen shyoo," this is a simple, commonplace name. Xiu means "elegant."

Page 65 **Lao Jin**: the word Lao, literally "old" or "venerable," is commonly used in China along with the surname of a senior co-worker as an informal but respectful form of address.

Page 66 **Chengdu**: capital city of Sichuan Province.

Page 68 **Sky burial**: a traditional Tibetan ritual through which the remains of the dead are returned to the elements. The body of the deceased is taken to a deserted place and, after the appropriate preparations and prayers, placed on an elevated platform and left to the birds to devour.

Page 81 **Caterpillar grass**: this type of grass, which when dried resembles a bunch of caterpillars, is used in Chinese herbal medicine as a tonic.

Page 82 **Mournful white**: white, rather than black, is the traditional color of mourning in China.

Page 84 **Immortal**: sometimes translated "fairies," the Immortals are the popular saints and demigods of Taoist folk religion.

少尉之死　The Death of the Lieutenant

At first, when a piercing, exaggerated voice called for "the accused," the lieutenant did not know it was calling for him. He was no longer his old self, the one with that name so bumpkinlike it embarrassed him—the self whose smell of peasant mud it had taken four years of military academy to remove; the self that with two stiff rectangles on the shoulders could make thirty-odd young soldiers hold down their burps, hold in their farts and hold eye contact while they addressed him with "Yes, sir, Platoon Leader!"

Only when the voice once again bounced around the four walls, dragging along names of people and affairs apparently connected with him, did he pull himself together with a start: I am "the accused." This appellation spiraled upward, and suddenly he felt the ceiling had ascended much higher, but, like the big temple he saw when he was a little boy, its height pressed down on his shortness.

I am the accused. He slowly raised his eyes and resigned himself to this meekly. So that's what "the accused" is: a head full of uneven hair, two acrid-smelling armpits, a face as white as a big toe stuffed too long inside rainboots. Almost everyone was seated but him. Also standing were two soldiers in full battle regalia. Behind him they stood, or were held upright, by martial bearing, dignity, justice. On the prisoner transport they had in no way shown him a tiger's face; rather they had been calm, indifferent, their faces stripped of all expression. Yet because of this calm indifference, he breathed very carefully, for fear that even a slight movement would break it.

As his gaze panned upward, the first thing he saw was a white nameplate engraved with the black characters "Presiding Judge." Evenly, one by one, the black characters hammered his eyes. He soon discovered that they had hammered into his consciousness.

The lieutenant also discovered his mouth was half open, the way country cousins look at a spectacle, look at a stranger, look at the occasional airplane that climbs the skies, their two lips gaping open. *This just won't do.* With effort he drew his lower lip back up, but the strain set his teeth to chattering. Then, after a while, his lower lip lost all strength; again it separated from the upper lip and drooped, just like all the other limbs of his body. Were it not for the floor supporting them, they would all endlessly droop down, drop down. So it was that, as the object of that strange form of address "the accused," the lieutenant reverted to his original villager's demeanor, to his original form.

I am the accused. The lieutenant of half a year ago—cussing people merrily, whistling as he pissed, so happy whenever he received a letter from Momo that his whole body would tingle—was gone. Now the one standing here, breathing like a human being, was "the accused." Who is accusing me? That fellow Wang Youquan who died without uttering a word? Wang, the supply officer whose mouth was always either spouting nonsense or else drawn together like a healed wound? No, not him. When he fell, the only sound that came from his throat was a faint gurgling, probably his lungs pushing out a string of beer bubbles.

"The accused Liu Liangku, male, age twenty-five, formerly lieutenant and platoon leader in the X autonomous unit of Y regiment, native of Liu Village in Ding County, Shanxi Province . . ." Enough. That's enough to figure out all the rest. No need to tell how steep the stone hedges are that separate the fields there, carving out a strip of land no wider than a pair of buttocks. No matter what grows on that strip, it has to fill people's mouths and bellies. Father would lead the way, digging up yams as big as feet, Mother would pick up the ones as big as fists, while the children would pull out those the size of fingers. And not a single yam shoot was thrown away. When the wok was empty, the shoots would be its only contents. They would be swallowed down whole, complete with stems and leaves, and they would pass through the bowels with stems and leaves still attached. The lieutenant still remembered how those things swept relentlessly through his extremely thin stomach and intestines, scrubbing away any remnants of beautiful memories or yearnings connected with eating.

Momo was the fourth daughter in her family. When she was born, her father's already long face dragged even longer as he told her terribly chagrined mother, "It would have been better if you'd borne me a chaff bun *(momo)*." Later, when Momo came to the barracks to see the lieutenant, she wrinkled her face and complained, "Why do you still call me 'Bun' now that you have buns to eat every day? Can't you see the way those soldiers are laughing themselves silly?"

"So what kind of a name *do* you want?"

"You're asking *me?* So which one of us went to the county seat for high school, and who went on to military academy?"

When he caught the soldiers laughing again, he said, "Go ahead and laugh, you bastards." By then he could halfway use Beijing slang to curse. "Her name is Momò! Momò—ink, symbolizing a craving for knowledge!" For the past several years, the newspapers had been covered from end to end with phrases like "Seek knowledge," "Self-study promotes skill" and other such slogans.

"On May 8, 1987, the criminal Liu Liangku trespassed onto the premises of the military supply warehouse . . ."

Trespassed. Military supply warehouse. Suddenly he raised his eyes and scanned all the faces before him, as if searching for someone with whom to discuss the difference between "trespassing" and "barging in," and whether these two words carried the same severe connotation. I just took advantage of no one being there to enter soundlessly, right? Besides, it wasn't the military supply warehouse; it was just a little room next to the warehouse, right?

The lieutenant's gaze finally came to rest on the face of a woman. Her face was smaller than all the others, small as a child's. Only a child's face could be so clean, so unable to conceal surprise, so unable to avoid his unabashed eyes desperately seeking to understand. *I didn't do all that on purpose.* I didn't think Supply Officer Wang would return so soon. I didn't expect my hand would be that heavy. Even at my age, I've never been in a real fight. I'm not a mean person. Even in the military academy, when the meanest drill instructor punished me with a five-kilometer run with full pack, I only aimed my rifle at him in my mind. I never did anything to him. He used to abuse all the young recruits from the village, saying we were as dumb as fresh cow dung. Even at the graduation ceremony, he was still laughing and poking my stomach, saying, "Dammit, boy! It wasn't that long ago your dad sent you here—the year of the bad grain crop. But this military academy has got one fine mess hall, and you really shot up after you got here. Look at you, you sure have grown a lot, haven't you?" He had come so close that with one good punch I could have crushed his face like a watermelon, sending its red and white parts flying in all directions. But in the end I didn't touch a hair on his head. I really didn't know that Supply Officer Wang's life could be snuffed out just like that. Look at me, do I look like someone who could just kill somebody without flinching . . .?

The childlike woman had been looking at him the whole time. Only when the lieutenant became uneasy from the woman's gaze did he drop his eyes. After a while, he raised them again. She was still looking at him that way, both hands balled into fists squeezing her face, lightly suspending the skin of her cheeks and eyes, both elbows resting on the table, a pile of paper in front of her. He couldn't see clearly whether the paper was blank or if something was written on it. She just kept looking at him like that. *Everyone is looking at me like that.* He was netted right in everyone's line of sight. He dared not move a muscle. But she was different. He felt her difference was not just because she was the only woman at these proceedings or because she was the only person not in uniform. *All right, go ahead and look.* The way she stared at him made the lieutenant feel she was not merely looking at him but reading him, reading his mind, reading his thoughts. It seemed that his wickedness and cruelty required all her effort, for she focused on him without distraction. Didn't he himself feel there was some part of him that was hidden and hard to understand? Didn't he himself wonder how he could have stopped suddenly on his way to the barracks and dashed soundlessly to the right, like a wildcat? To the right was the little path that led to Supply Officer Wang's independent kingdom. In it was a refrigerator and a television set. The base commander and his wife often emerged from that door making beer burps. The supply officer's bedroom, which doubled as his office, was next to a series of food-ration storerooms. Inside them were piled boxes of condensed high-nutrition biscuits from the 1960s, tinned camp rations from the 1970s and sacks of flour and rice and bundles of air-dried jerky from the 1980s.

The lieutenant saw that the first page of the record of his misdeeds had finally been turned. At most they would turn two more pages until they reached the page with the round red stamp on it. He saw a spot of red mist showing through the back of the last page. When they'd put on that seal, they must have gorged it on thick red ink, or else they pressed too hard. The lieutenant knew that his fate was pressed into that red spot. It was a red and forgone conclusion.

But what could the conclusion be? A few decades at hard labor? A sentence never to see Momo again for the rest of his life? Would Momo look for some way to come see him? No, she would not. She would marry someone else and rub that downy forehead of hers against someone else's neck and point to a gold necklace as thick as a flax thread in the jewelry case and ask disingenuously, "What's that?"

"It's something we can't afford," the lieutenant had told her at the time.

"If you can't afford it, then I don't want it!"

"You really don't want it?"

"No!"

"Well, then, shall we go? Why are you still staring at it?" Momo tossed her head. "What do you mean 'we'? You go your way. I know I can't afford it, but does that mean I can't afford to look?"

It was at that moment that the lieutenant discovered Momo's face had become unfamiliar—flatter and wider than the face he knew, with a yellow nose tip. This was because seeping sweat had washed off all the powder. And when did Momo learn to apply face powder? After coming to Beijing? From Youhui, the base commander's wife, who works in the barber shop? Youhui's neck and fingers were dripping with gold, even though she was only half a city person. But how could the lieutenant compare himself to the base commander? The base commander didn't have a family that surrounded a wok eating black yam leaves. He didn't have a mother who was unable to stop bleeding ever since she had borne her last child. He didn't have an elder brother who wanted a wife so badly it drove him crazy.

Momo knew how things were. When he saw her off, when she was in the train and he was on the platform, she said she wouldn't ask anything of him. If he had money, he should spare his family from having to eat another meal of yam leaves. She smiled and became the original Momo, but it seemed as if one small movement could shatter this impression.

"Momo, when I have money . . . I'll give you something else. That gold chain is just too expensive."

"Who needs it? It's so thick you could tether an ox with it!" Momo wrinkled her nose and drew her mouth into a straight line, breaking her smile.

The mouth hidden behind the paper continued to reveal the lieutenant's transgressions, spitting them out word by word. ". . . After the criminal Liu's theft was discovered, he developed murderous intentions. Picking up a weighted practice hand grenade, he hurled it right on target toward Supply Officer Wang Youquan's cranial area . . ."

The lieutenant gave a start, suddenly recognizing that this hideous diabolical thing was actually himself. He did not dare, did not want to accept—and only did so reluctantly—that all of this was not someone else. It was undeniably himself. Just like his undeniably impoverished family, impoverished ancestors and the impoverished land that had raised him.

"Stand up straight!" Behind him, a hand stretched out to yank his shoulder. As he winced, the lieutenant knew that no one else could see how much secret venom was in that yank.

And yet the woman seemed to understand. She had just been tapping the tip of her pen against her lips, and suddenly she stopped tapping. The tip of the pen remained fixed to her lower lip, stilled, while her eyes captured the full revelation of his pain. They registered her gradually expanding terror, as it became clear to her that his shoulder had collapsed to a different level, that it had secretly been dislocated.

The lieutenant's previously half-open mouth closed. All he could do to resist the excruciating pain was to hold every breath. *I'd better sleep on my left side tonight.* He wondered how long it would take for the injured arm to recover the ability to use chopsticks, buckle his belt buckle and button his buttons. The lieutenant felt a bead of sweat slowly, slowly gather on the tip of his nose. It seemed that his flesh, painful to the point of dissolving, would drain completely away in this viscous sweat.

"Wang Youquan sustained a massive injury to the head area and instantly lost consciousness. Two hours later, after futile attempts to revive him . . . he was pronounced dead."

When the lieutenant heard the word "dead" read out so unfeelingly, he almost started to feel emotional about Supply Officer Wang. Even though, in life, Wang Youquan didn't dole out full measure from the food supplies under his stewardship but kept them to curry favor with the base commander and his wife as well as that high-heeled girlfriend of his whose butt stuck out when she walked, still he did not deserve death. If the lieutenant hadn't noticed him that day, going out of his way to send off "High Heels," reluctant to see her go, the lieutenant would never have slipped into his room.

But of course, if the lieutenant hadn't missed the train home to visit his family that day, none of that would have had an opportunity to occur. Actually, the lieutenant shouldn't have missed the train in the first place. That day he had started out early in the morning, even though the train didn't leave until the afternoon. He had advanced and retreated through all the shops, large and small, of Wangfujing, Dongdan and Xidan, trying to think of something to buy for Momo. From silk stockings to hair ornaments, from skirts to overcoats, he rubbed and kneaded them all between his fingers. But then he would rub the wad of bills in his pocket, and his whole body would break into a sweat. Finally, in a little privately owned shop, he saw a pair of dangling earrings. He had no idea whether the two little bright things that looked like a thief's eyes were pretty or not. He just knew that all the women on the street were wearing them, including the base commander's wife Youhui.

"Forty-eight *yuan.*"

"Are they . . . gold?"

"For forty-eight *yuan* you want to buy *gold?* These are rhinestones!"

"Please don't put them back just yet. Let me look at them a little while longer!"

"You can look at them, but no touching. If you finger them like that, I'm afraid you'll break them."

The lieutenant didn't heed the salesgirl's smiling, barbed talk. Such a little thing it was—drop it on the ground and it's gone, yet it costs a half a hundred! Half a hundred worth of corn flour would fill up the bellies of everyone in the family for ten days. Once, when he went on home leave, he brought two bags of onion and oil cakes that he had bought at a breakfast stand and invited Momo's family over to eat together with his. After they had finished off both bags, everybody's belly looked like someone had stuck a big bowl on top of it. And he had only paid ten yuan for all of it. After the meal, he and Momo walked into the cornfield. He turned his head and, seeing that Momo's belly had shape and form and stuck out like a bowl, he laughed out loud. Momo laughed as well. A person who hasn't eaten his fill absolutely cannot laugh like that. Suddenly, like a bandit, he pinned Momo with his arms. Momo showed no weakness, and when she fell, she purposely dragged him down with her. But he didn't dare to behave any more banditlike, because he had just become a lieutenant and still couldn't support Momo. Nevertheless, Momo's face was still under his neck looking like a baby waiting to be nursed, her fists kneading into his armpits vigorously. By then, his body temperature was at the boiling point.

"Momo, this is just wonderful, just wonderful . . ."

Momo's two thick round legs locked around him, and at the same time she grabbed his hand and placed it on her breast. Suddenly, an idea came to him: if you took off a city girl's skirt and high heels, there probably wouldn't be much of anything left inside. What a contrast to Momo—wherever your hand touched, it would come up with a handful. Not just a handful: her youth, her fullness, her truly feminine insinuations seemed as if they would flow out between your fingers. Momo made his chest fill to the bursting point. It cost him great effort to quell her playful passion. After the mad desire had passed, she sighed toward the stars above and said, "I don't want those gold or silver things, and I don't want nice clothes, colorful head scarves or sheer stockings. I just want you. If I'm with you, it's better than good, more than enough."

"What about high heels?"

"Don't want those either. With those pointy little heels poking into the cornfield, they'd have to plant me along with the corn!"

But the lieutenant knew that actually she wanted him, and she also wanted nice clothes, colorful head scarves, and sheer stockings as well as high heels. The lieutenant was well aware that Momo coveted Supply Officer Wang's girlfriend's high-heeled shoes. Otherwise she wouldn't have gone to the county seat to learn how to raise rabbits, nor would she have permitted that rabbit pelt buyer from Taiyuan to harbor wicked intentions toward her. The rabbit pelt buyer had been sweet-talking her, saying he had enough money with him to marry ten Momos, enough to buy Momo residence permits in ten cities. Momo wrote the lieutenant a letter saying she hated the buyer, and she hated herself. Hated the fact that she had no blood relatives outside this desolate place, hated the poverty that had grown into her flesh, blood and bones.

The lieutenant also felt the same hatred. When Supply Officer Wang slapped down his bag of pay in front of him, that hatred shook his whole being. "Your salary for this month is twelve *yuan*. There's nothing to be done about it. According to the regulations, I had to start making deductions to pay back your salary advances. Last year you took an advance of one thousand *yuan* that hasn't been paid back yet, and this year you borrowed five hundred again. I know your family lives in hardship. They have to fix the house, get medical treatment, buy grain. Still, I can't change the regulations. You know as well as I do that salary advances are only good for a limited period. If they haven't been repaid on time, then we have to make severe deductions like this. Twelve *yuan* a month will cover the mess hall. You're on your own for movies, cigarettes and such." Supply Officer Wang's hand held the remote control of his TV, and he stared at the screen as he said to the lieutenant, "Aren't the villages reforming these days? Hasn't your family reformed itself a little richer?" The lieutenant replied that his place was poor. Anything that was planted in that poor soil came out poor.

Now the lieutenant, standing accused before the court, thought it was precisely that poverty that had stripped off in an instant his righteousness and innocence. From the moment of his birth, he lost all rights, including even the right to rid himself of his poverty.

"The criminal Liu Liangku's thoughts had for some time been subject to the influence of bourgeois thinking. He was infatuated with the bourgeois lifestyle . . ."

The lieutenant cautiously shook his head, as if to take issue with this judgmental statement, and also to make himself stand up with more dignity. But the pain in his shoulder checked him and reminded him that the life he was to lead from now on would be that of a second-class citizen. This second-class status would prevent him from taking issue with many things. Just like his family's old ox with its bones protruding through its hide. The only reason it lived was because people allowed it to live. His father never ceased cursing it: "Half-breed! Dog-fuck! Slacking off with the load? You deserve to be whipped! Slaughtered!" It would simply avert its eyes from this foul poisonous language, closing them, then opening them.

The lieutenant felt his own eyes become dully obedient. From the moment they had snapped the handcuffs on him, he knew that at least thirty years of life as a beast awaited him—waited in that big red seal on the last page. Perhaps it would be a life sentence. Then he would live the whole rest of his life as a beast and die as one. Would they sentence him to a delayed death sentence? An execution by firing squad delayed for two years—allowing the terror to fill every minute of those two years before your body was annihilated—letting your spirit and consciousness die minute by minute. That cruelty would far exceed the rap he had given to Supply Officer Wang's head.

"The criminal's methods were brutal, and the details of the crime are heinous . . ." Step by step, the theatrical monotone of the voice was approaching that big red seal.

Oddly, he felt a moment of dead calm come over the courtroom. This calm was intimidating. Everyone remained motionless in uneasy awkward postures, including the woman. She was preparing to stand up and leave her seat, but she stopped her movements midway. Everyone knew that something was about to happen . . . everyone except the lieutenant in question. The woman looked at him, and her eyes met his. Her eyes gave a shudder, then she suppressed it. She must know the answer to the riddle in the red seal! She must have conspired with everyone else on his punishment! She must have come to understand the incident through and through and concluded he was a type for whom bloodthirstiness had been second nature from birth. She must know what kind of outcome awaited him.

Like Momo in the train window, talking and laughing and saying goodbye to him—yet looking at him with sighing eyes. When his eyes met Momo's, she averted hers, because she knew that in the end she would not be able to face him, that she would betray him. In Momo's eyes he could read urging and coercion. He must act, must do something, otherwise in the end he would not have this Momo whose whole body was good. He started to scrimp and save. Since he only had twelve *yuan* a month, he used twenty *fen* a day to buy a pound of *mantou* which he split into three meals. He would pour on top of it a bowl of bouillon that the mess hall provided free of charge, or skin broth, or rice broth. Sometimes it was just a basin of muddy-colored water. That was when there was no broth and the kitchen just took the oil from the wok where the food had been cooked, brushed and scraped it out, added some soy sauce, dumped in a scallion flower and called it "broth." After a year, on the early morning of the day he was to go on home leave, he had carried in his bosom one hundred *yuan* he had saved in this manner and had scoured the city for the nice clothes, colorful head scarves and long sheer stockings that Momo claimed she "didn't like." But always, when the moment finally came to pay, he would take to his heels. He had used up a whole day yet preserved the entire hundred *yuan* in his uniform pocket without parting with a single *fen*. He even used up the time he needed to take a bus to the train station. Toward evening, he returned to the barracks. On the little pathway outside the gate, he ran into Supply Officer Wang, stuck to the side of his girlfriend. "Huh?" Wang said. "Aren't you supposed to be away on home leave?"

He smiled through his fatigue and told him he had missed the train. He had changed his ticket to the following day.

When the lieutenant walked into Supply Officer Wang's office-bedroom next to the supply warehouse, he didn't yet realize he was walking into crime, with no exit and no turning back. He did not notice his fingers had already become ruthless and deft. When they picked the lock, they did so as beautifully as if he were a natural-born thief. The supply officer's TV was still on, but the sound had been turned off. The naked baby boy on the screen, crying hysterically with his mouth wide open, was obviously a focus of life's misfortunes. The baby boy wept and yelled as he was gradually carried off into the distance in a sampan. The boatman's single oar pole cast a long dark shadow behind it. On the shore, a woman was also crying, craning her neck and calling to the baby boy off in the distance. Their mouths and faces moved vigorously, yet there was not a sound. The heart-rending sorrow of this silent scene—this silent screaming to the point of exhaustion—reached its highest pitch just as he cracked open the lock on the drawer. Inside were just a few stray bills that hadn't yet been entered into the accounts. The lieutenant grabbed them and stuffed them into his pockets. They're not much, he thought, but they're enough to buy something that Momo desires. Apparently, he had a thief's intuition as well as a thief's deftness. That intuition cut short his desire to force open the other drawer. He must leave immediately. It wouldn't be long before the woman and the little boy on the screen would call back Supply Officer Wang with their soundless screams.

The lieutenant had heard of fingerprints, but since he'd had no time to find a pair of gloves, he used a towel to cover his fingers while he did his work. He even planned to take the screwdriver he'd used to pick the lock and throw it from the window of the train. As far as he could tell, he hadn't left fingerprints on anything.

Raising his head up as he finished his business, the lieutenant was startled by the woman on the TV. The woman's face took up all twenty-four inches of the screen. Her wide-open mouth seemed to show him its full depth, that red dark abyss. He couldn't remember whether in that moment he hesitated, caught red-handed by the clinking sound of Supply Officer Wang's heel studs announcing his approach. There wasn't enough time to run away. The best thing was to walk out and meet him face to face. Hey, I've been waiting for you; I wanted to see if I could get a little more pay advance for home leave. He could use an excuse like this. The worst that could happen is that Supply Officer Wang would make an even grumpier face than usual, that he would have to listen to even meaner talk. Look at you, going in without being invited. He could get by with a brazen face: I saw your door wasn't locked, so I thought I'd come in and watch a little TV. Sir, your TV is bigger than the one at headquarters, and much better. If Supply Officer Wang heard him talk like this, he might start to relax.

But how to explain that drawer and his pocket stuffed recklessly with bills? In a minute, Supply Officer Wang would catch on and call out, "Hey, you!" and after that, there would be no getting around it. To prevent this "Hey, you!" from happening, as soon as Supply Officer Wang's clinking heel plates crossed the threshold, the lieutenant, like the outstanding cadet he had once been, would have to leap sideways and dodge behind the door. Then, with the skilled judgment of a commander, he would determine the method and direction of his escape. Behind the door lay some training hand grenades that Supply Officer Wang used for working out, to beautify his muscles. They were just heavy enough, the lieutenant estimated. Not heavy enough to take Wang's life, but heavy enough so he wouldn't make any noise and would lie there properly for a while. He would take advantage of Wang's obliviousness to count the money and put it all back, then fix the lock. As long as the cash count wasn't short, no one would notice a slight change in the lock. As for Supply Officer Wang—if seventy percent of the troops wanted to knock off the base commander, then the percentage who wanted to knock *him* off was higher still. On what basis would they suspect an honest straightforward lieutenant? At most it would be viewed as a case of personal revenge. And it might even cause them to scrutinize Supply Officer Wang's unaccountable affluence. It was said that the big television set had been acquired by bartering canned military rations that had passed their expiration date. Afterward, there might even be secret rejoicing among the soldiers: "Supply Officer Wang sure deserved getting clubbed by that fellow. That's how he found out that it doesn't taste so good to suck soldiers' blood!"

When the door opened, the lieutenant could discern Supply Officer Wang's white hand in the darkness, stretching toward the light switch next to the door. He absolutely could not allow him to see or understand anything before falling down. The lieutenant, taking advantage of his superior height, watched as the practice hand grenade formed a very short, but very beautiful trajectory. The lieutenant repaired the lock and put back all the money, looked at Supply Officer Wang's properly supine posture, then walked out the door. He didn't return to his barracks but went to a half-finished construction site near the base and sat down. He just sat there dumbfounded, with his back against the wall, until his buttocks hurt and his spine went numb; then he finally stood up. He decided to get the last bus into town; then he'd take the early morning train back home. On the narrow paved road that led from the city toward the barracks, a screeching ambulance brushed past him. It was rushing toward Supply Officer Wang. Apparently Supply Officer Wang had suffered unforeseen consequences from that blow. *No one will suspect me.* If Wang Youquan dies, there is absolutely no one who knows I missed the train and came back. Everyone would come under suspicion but me—I'm the only one they could rule out. But I hope he doesn't die. If he dies, there's going to be a big fuss.

When he returned from home leave, all the other soldiers he met raised their eyebrows, crooked their mouths, squinted their eyes and snorted, telling him, "Supply Officer Wang 'honorably made the supreme sacrifice.' Everyone's been interrogated. Boy, are you lucky—the exact same day you left the base for home leave, that night somebody clubbed him to death."

"Was there any money missing?" the lieutenant asked. As soon as he asked, he realized he was compromising himself.

"Nope. The military security officers opened the drawer, and not a red cent was missing. That old guy sure won't be kissing the base commander's ass *now!*"

That evening the lieutenant was conducted to the base headquarters. The base commander was standing with both hands clasped behind his back, looking out the window. Two military security officers had usurped both the base commander's and the political commissar's desks. The lieutenant thought to himself: I took the hand grenade murder weapon and the screwdriver on the train with me, wrapped them in newspaper and threw them out the window of the train. You can forget about fingerprints or any evidence like that.

"When was the last time you saw Wang Youquan?"

"The day before I went on home leave. I got some travel expenses over at his place and picked up the train ticket he had ordered for me."

"Was anyone else present?"

"No."

"What time was it?"

"Two-thirty in the afternoon."

"What was he doing at the time?"

"He was on the phone. He asked me to wait a while."

"How long did you wait?"

"I'm . . . not sure."

"What did you do while you were waiting?"

"I watched TV."

"At two-thirty in the afternoon during duty hours, Wang Youquan had the TV on?"

"He always had the TV on—all the time."

"What program was on?"

"I don't know. He had the sound off. There was only a picture. It was a little boy crying and a young woman crying, too."

"Thank you. That will be all," the elder of the two military security officers said.

When the lieutenant stood up, his feet hit the floor with a "ka-chunk!" sound, and his heart thumped and fell back into its proper place.

During the interview, the base commander had not moved once. The entire time he had shown him his spine. Afterwards, when the lieutenant had left and was taking an alternate route to the parade grounds, he turned his head and saw the big window at base headquarters and the base commander's face, expressionless as a wood carving, his eyes angled slightly upward like a dead horse's. Apparently he was terribly sorrowful about Supply Officer Wang's death, only it wasn't clear whether he was mourning the supply officer himself or the practical benefits the supply officer had afforded him.

That same night the lieutenant was roused from a very deep sleep and marched back to the base commander's office. Under a snow-bright lamp, he saw the two security officers sitting in the same places as before and the base commander standing with his hands scissored behind his back, only this time the commander was facing him. His eyes still looked like those of a dead horse, but now they were fixed on him. To be stared at like that by that kind of a dead thing made the lieutenant's hair stand on end.

"We'll give you another chance," one of the security officers said. "Tell us the truth: when *really* was the last time you saw Wang Youquan?"

" . . . The day before my home leave."

"Do you want me to repeat the question?"

The lieutenant turned his eyes toward the base commander but realized then he was the least likely to come to his aid.

"Answer the question!"

"Ah . . .?!" the lieutenant felt his consciousness blown away with a "wha!" sound, scattered to the four winds.

Having gotten shorter and shorter the longer he stood before the judge, the lieutenant tried to pull himself up. It will be over soon, he told himself. It will be over soon. He thought of the woman, and again he raised his eyes searching for her, wanting to find out. She looked at him, then she looked behind him at the future that would follow him. So she did not see him at all. Just as when Momo leaned out the doorway of her house, propping herself against the half-open door, her wrist bearing a bright thing with delicate sparkles that pierced his eyes. She looked at him, yet did not see him; rather she saw trailing behind him his debts, his poverty and his family that would always need to be fed. He could squeeze himself dry, but it still wouldn't remedy anything. Too late. He had come rushing back with a hundred *yuan* and a crime on his head, but it was still too late.

The gold chain on her wrist explained that someone else had beaten him to it and chained her up. They just stood there facing each other. She couldn't so much as work up a smile, and in the end he couldn't muster enough strength to ask her a single question.

" . . . The accused has admitted to and in no way contested the foregoing account of his crime. In light of this court's investigation and verification, and in accordance with military justice, we have determined the following sentence: we condemn the thief and murderer Liu Liangku to death, the sentence to be carried out summarily!"

The lieutenant's mouth dropped open, but he did not cry out. *Death! Sentence to be carried out summarily!* . . . A death sentence! Carried out summarily! What did that mean? Why was the lieutenant suddenly unable to understand these words, this type of language? The words traveled the four walls, circling round and round, brushing many times past the large blood red characters on the wall:

Lenience to those who confess;
Severity to those who resist.

Still the words echoed themselves, repeated themselves, like an uninterrupted cry in a dream, reverberating everywhere.

When the lieutenant came back to consciousness, he realized his face was full of tears and he was sobbing violently. The whole assembly was frozen in place, listening to his sobbing. The woman had stood up; she stared at him as if she had just received a fright.

"Didn't . . . didn't you," the Lieutenant heard his own voice broken by sobs. "Didn't you say if I confessed everything and told the truth, you guaranteed I wouldn't be sentenced to death? I . . . I believed you. I told the truth about everything. You didn't even have to go to the trouble of investigating; I told you everything that happened. I believed you! I *trusted* you . . . !"

The gavel sounded, "pah!" "If you hadn't told the truth, we still would have been able to determine the true state of affairs!" said the judge.

"You people said . . . 'leniency to those who confess . . .' "

"A murderer pays with his life, no matter whether he confesses or not."

"I . . . I didn't do it on purpose . . . I . . ."

"Enough of that!" the judge shouted him down. "Criminal Liu Liangku, this court has spoken. You have seven days in which to appeal. If you refuse to accept the decision of this court, you may appeal to a higher military court!"

The lieutenant brushed away a tear with his uninjured left arm and asked, "What does 'appeal' mean?"

"'Appeal' means you can have a legal advocate represent you before a higher legal authority to state the reasons for which you are dissatisfied with the original decision. After a week, if the appeal has been rejected, you will still be bound by the judgment rendered by this court. Do you understand?"

The lieutenant nodded his head. "What is a 'legal advocate'?"

"We can appoint an attorney for you."

"You . . . ?"

"That is correct."

"You . . ." The lieutenant slowly looked around at all the faces in the courtroom. Raising his eyes helplessly, he felt another wave of tears rushing forward but used all his strength to hold them back.

"Do I take that to mean that you waive your right to appeal?"

The lieutenant exerted effort to nod his head once.

"Well, then, before the death sentence is carried out, you may make a last request of the court. Criminal Liu Liangku, do you have a last request?"

The lieutenant lowered his eyes and face. "I would like to see my parents one last time."

"There is not enough time!"

Hearing this, the lieutenant felt suffocated. He had never imagined that his suffering and terror could be so great. Nor had he ever imagined he would be so loath to part with this short life full of hunger and privation. Even less had he imagined how much dearer his own life would be to him than Momo. After a moment of tumultuous thought, the lieutenant made several other requests, but each one was denied in turn. The only request granted was for a few sheets of paper and a pen. The night before his execution, he wanted to write a letter to his parents.

When it was dark, the lieutenant was locked into an individual cell for criminals sentenced to death. His feet were shackled to the end of his cot. He sat there with no thoughts. After a while, he lifted his wrist to look at his watch. Ten o'clock at night. Out of habit he began to wind his watch but stopped after two turns. There was no need. It was going to stop anyway. *After my life has stopped, it will still run for ten or more hours before it finally stops as well. But it can be restarted, be readjusted, and begin its circling again. Each of its rotations was so effortless, so unlike human affairs.*

At that point, he heard the sound of a key in the lock outside, then the sound of the iron bars opening. Presently a fully armed guard and the woman from the courtroom walked in. Her eyes were very wide. He had no desire to know who she was or why she had come. From now on, no one could ever have any significance for him or do him any harm. The woman walked forward a few steps, adjusting her facial expression several times. She told the guard, "Please let me talk with him alone. Just a little while."

The guard looked at the woman, apparently to see if she was entirely in her right mind. The lieutenant understood that the guard saw him as a wild beast. Even though it was tied up, such a beast could pose a threat for so slight a woman. The guard's expression was also worried, because death had already started its process in the lieutenant. Toward a thing that has already embarked on dying, is already partially dead, women are always half terrified and half disgusted. With these worries, the guard left the woman alone in the condemned prisoner's cell.

The lieutenant stared straight ahead at the wall, feeling something clean, carrying an odor of cleanliness, that gradually increased in the glaring bright light before his eyes.

"I'd like to talk with you," she said. "I'm a writer. I write novels."

Who cares what you do.

"Why did you give up your right to appeal? It was your last

chance. Maybe it could've turned the whole situation around!" she said urgently.

Little by little, he began to shake his head. His field of vision started to shake itself into muddy confusion. Her voice and speech were also shaken into confusion. She asked him what he was thinking at this moment. Injustice? Remorse? He answered everything with this dull exhausted shaking of the head. If he could have, he would have shaken off even this last bit of consciousness. He kept shaking his head, shaking until his death-row cell was still as death, shaking until this woman whose profession was to write about other people's pain and suffering saw her hopes die and did not bother him with another word.

He kept staring at the wall, waiting for her to leave. In the midst of his annoyed calm he thought, a person's whole life is actually full of things like this that try one's patience.

Finally she said she was leaving. He should write that letter to his parents. See you later.

See you later? His face remained unsmiling. When he heard the gate close, he turned his face. "You . . ." The lieutenant was amazed at his mouth's suddenly coming unsealed.

The woman writer turned back quickly from the cell door, her whole face and body nervous and agitated. "What do you want me to do for you? Don't miss this opportunity again! Maybe I can still do something in these last few hours!"

He looked at her. Or more precisely, he looked at her hands moving and moving as she talked to him. The lieutenant was disoriented for a moment, knowing by her short breaths that she was waiting for his response. He was still shaking his head. *No, don't trouble yourself.*

"You're worried that your mother, so weak and sick, won't be able to bear this news, aren't you?" Surprised, he stopped shaking his head. *She does read my thoughts.* On his last home leave, his mother had supported herself on a cane while seeing him off. He kept saying, Mother, go back. But his mother kept saying, I'll see you off a little farther, a little farther. It was early morning, and the dark sky still revealed a thin sliver of moon. He hadn't wanted to disturb anyone with his leaving, but when he stealthily groped his way into the yard, Mother was already waiting fully dressed by the gate. Just before they arrived at the main road, he said, Ma, once I've saved up some money, I'll bring you and Pa to Beijing to have a look. Mother seemed not to hear him. They walked on in silence for nearly half an hour. When he again pleaded with her not to go any farther, Mother stopped in her tracks. She waited until she could breathe a bit more easily, her eyes moving slowly from left to right, avoiding eye contact, then she told him: "Never come back again. This time, go back to your army unit and live your own life from now on. Momo is no longer yours, anyway. Don't let me worry you to death, drag you down to your death with this poor family. Look at this poor place. What do you want to come running back here for? A life lived is a life saved. Listen to your mother, never come back here. This time when you go, never in this life or in this world come back here again . . ." After she had finished, Mother went with him no further, nor did she watch him go off into the distance until she could no longer see him. Instead she turned around and walked back, very slowly but with great determination. If Mother knew he would really never return and knew the reason why, she wouldn't live long.

"They . . . they shouldn't have denied your request," the woman writer said. She was referring to the request he had had the most difficulty expressing to the court—the request that the officials conceal from his parents the fact that he had been executed. He had requested that they inform his folks only that he had died—died of foul play or died violently, even, but just not tell them he died because he broke the law.

"Sometimes the law is as cruel as crime," the woman writer said. He turned his face back toward her and saw her neat figure set off by the lead-colored iron door. A dense feeling of loneliness welled up inside him: how far removed she was from crime! The door sounded with a metallic clang as it shut.

When the clang of the opening door came again, he put down his pen. All through the night, he had used his uninjured left hand to fill the four sheets of paper he had been issued. He still had much to say, but he had no more time and no more paper left.

The lieutenant watched the two guards walk in. He instinctively recoiled and at the same time thought how stupid this recoiling was. There was no point in resisting. He didn't say anything like, "Don't carry me, let me walk myself," because he had no confidence that he would be able to stand and walk. His legs were trembling severely; it was best just to let them tremble. He also knew he had that half-open mouth that so disgusted everyone, and there was a frozen string of saliva suspended between his upper and lower teeth, but he could no longer control this.

Eight fully armed guards were waiting in front of the prisoner transport. Surprisingly, the woman writer was also there. Her mouth was pursed tightly and she avoided looking in his direction. The guards stuffed him unceremoniously into the transport, dumping him onto the floor in the back. Then they sat down, one next to the other, on the two opposing benches inside. He faced the tail of the transport, kneeling between the two rows of feet. One of the soldiers stretched out a helping hand to the woman writer waiting outside. She leaned her body forward, but in the end she didn't get in. "I'm not going to the execution grounds," she said. "You go ahead."

For a moment the lieutenant raised his head. She was looking at him, her eyes swollen with two large tears. The lieutenant couldn't be certain he saw clearly those were tears in her eyes, couldn't be certain what had caused them—pity, injustice? Perhaps those tears were just one life saying to another life, "Farewell."

After a while, the lieutenant was taken out of the transport and plopped down shapelessly on a plot of muddy ground. He couldn't determine whether he was kneeling or sitting, or if he was simply piled there. The transport and guards that had brought him left quickly after unloading him, and immediately a severe-looking military truck drove up, completely masked with canvas. An entire nest of soldiers jumped out, wearing military rain ponchos and rain hats, their mouths covered by large surgical masks, leaving only pairs of black eyes exposed. He understood: every poncho hid one rifle.

Behind his back, they relayed their orders in whispers.

"It's still five minutes to four," a voice said.

The lieutenant opened his eyes and used his last five minutes of life to look once more at the sky and the earth. There was a little point of pink between earth and sky. A little higher was the yellow morning star. Higher still, there was a thin sliver of moon, just like the one he saw when Mother said, "Don't come back."

Then came a huge noise. The lieutenant did not feel this noise as coming from outside; rather it was a roar coming from inside his body. Along with the noise, he felt he had suddenly been magnified. Another sound came, and he saw the sky and the earth splattered with huge drops of blood.

The lieutenant saw his own death. Just as he saw the sky, earth, stars and moon, so could he witness his own death with blood splattered in all directions.

A long time later, he saw a woman's shadow slowly walk up to the muddy field where his bones and ashes were buried. It was Momo. A little closer and he realized he was mistaken: she looked more like that woman writer. And yet she wasn't. Finally he determined it was his mother. This was his mother of more than twenty years ago. Back then, she was young, had just given birth to him and saw him as a bundle of hope being born on this earth.

He used a blade of grass to whistle a lingering raucous sound, just as he had done in his childhood. He thought she heard him, because she suddenly looked about expectantly, near and far. Then she said, "Never come back again. Never come back again." She pressed her voice very low, because this was only for him to hear; it was enough that he alone should hear it.

The woman writer locked herself indoors for many days. When she came out, she told people she hadn't written anything because she couldn't figure out at all what had gone through the mind of the condemned lieutenant.

"He was really young, too young. I just remember the way he cried. When he heard he was sentenced to death, he burst into tears and cried just like a child." She recalled with effort: "He was completely calm from head to toe. It was a kind of primitive compliant calm. That's right, he still hadn't finished writing that letter to his parents when the time came to carry out the sentence. In the last character square of the last line, he wrote three dots, showing he couldn't continue, then he also wrote three little dots in the first square of the next line, completing a proper ellipsis, just like in primary school, the way your teacher tells you to do it."

As to her indescribable distress when she saw the transport carry him to the execution grounds and her sudden tears at the last sight of the young lieutenant, she mentioned nothing.

The woman writer shrugged her hands listlessly: "What is there to write about? If I wrote it, it would just be a very commonplace, very simple story, without even the slightest bit of intrigue."

Notes to "The Death of the Lieutenant"

Page 88 **Wang Youquan:** pronounced approximately "wong yo-chyhen." The characters for the given name mean "have" or "possession" plus "spring" or "source."

Page 88 **Liu Liangku:** the characters for the lieutenant's given name (pronounced "lyang koo") mean "grain storage."

Page 88 **Liu village:** since traditionally in China women go to live with the man's family and take his surname, it is not uncommon in remote areas for everyone in the village to belong to the same clan and have the same surname, as in Lieutenant Liu's village.

Page 89 **"Momo...so what kind of name *do* you want?":** because Chinese personal names are fairly unique creations based on the numerous ideographs of the language, educated people were traditionally called upon to devise names.

Page 89 **Momò:** the syllable "mò" pronounced in a different tone means "ink."

Page 94 **Foregone conclusion:** in a Chinese court, the judge has both investigative and judicial powers, and most matters are decided in advance of the trial. The court official is reading out the results of the investigation, which will conclude with the verdict and the sentence.

Page 94 **Wangfujing, Dongdan, Xidan:** major shopping areas of Beijing.

Page 94 **Yuan:** the currency unit of China, which is divided into one hundred *fen*. In the late 1980s, 48 *yuan* was half a factory worker's monthly pay.

Page 98 **Mantou:** a dense, steamed sourdough wheat staple similar to bread.

Page 111 **Proper ellipsis:** Chinese writing paper is often marked with squares in which to write each individual character. A properly written Chinese ellipsis has six dots, three each filling two squares of the writing paper.

紅 蘋 果 Red Apples

TRANSLATOR'S NOTE: *This story takes place in Tibet during the Cultural Revolution, when Tibet had been under Chinese Communist rule for about twenty years. The young Chinese travelers depicted here are part of the People's Liberation Army, which included performing arts troupes made up of teenagers from urban areas. The purpose of these troupes was to provide entertainment and boost morale among the Chinese soldiers stationed in Tibet.*

When we started up the mountain, the sky was clear; then, after three or four bends in the road, the fog was thick as sour milk. By the time we reached the top, the sky was white. Our driver, who had been rattling along the dirt roads of the Sichuan-Tibet frontier for many years, stopped the canvas-topped truck. Even he raised his head and looked around, saying, "How can the sky be so white?"

All of us girl soldiers jumped out of the truck. We had ridden the whole way with our knees pressed together, since there had been no latrine, and the driver had ignored our loud complaints that we were about to burst. We ran about half a kilometer away. Four or five of us took off our leather overcoats, formed a circle with our backs to each other and held our coats in front of ourselves with both hands. Everyone took turns using the empty space in the middle of the circle. The long robes the Tibetan women wear have certain advantages: squat down, then stand up, and everything is taken care of quite nicely.

We ran back to find the boy soldiers waiting impatiently. "What did you think you'd find running all the way out there?" they yelled. "A flush toilet?"

As the truck slowly started to move again, a young woman appeared at the bend in the road. "Get a ride?" she asked. Many Tibetans do not speak Chinese, but they all know this phrase. She wasn't looking at us directly but stood there turning her body slightly to the left and right in what seemed a combination of girlish pride and world-weariness. The whole truck yelled out, "Stop!" At last someone got up the courage to give voice to our thoughts. "That Tibetan girl is really pretty!"

Along the route, we had seen Tibetan women pounding barley and churning yak butter. When they felt hot, they would roll their robes down to their waists. Two shapeless things on their chests would shake about busily, as if wanting to help out. After a while, we began to forget they were women.

But this young woman was different. She was wearing a long one-piece robe of inky green. If it hadn't been so dirty, it would probably have been emerald. Her shoulders, neck and chin were delicate and slender. When two of the boys got down to lift her in, she stuck her chin forward and stretched out both hands in front of herself. Someone broke the silence again. "She's blind!"

We helped her into the truck and put her in the corner along with her shallow wooden bucket of red apples. Her face turned from side to side as if she were looking around inside and outside the truck, and all of us inside the truck were just part of the scenery. She appeared to be about twenty-six or twenty-seven, but by then we knew that Tibetan women generally looked about ten years older than their actual ages. She was probably only seventeen.

When we got to the Yajiang military way station, she went off by herself.

The Yajiang way station has two large hot springs. As soon as we heard we could take a bath, we all let out a loud "Hooray!" Ever since we'd entered Tibet, we'd been so dirty that we felt heavy. Some of the veteran soldiers told us that after serving in Tibet a few years, they developed an oily film all over their bodies. If a grain of barley dropped into our navels, they said, it would be sure to sprout.

After the hot springs had been taken over by the military, they had put walls around them, dug two deep pools and lined them with cement. Whenever a regional commander or someone of similar rank entered Tibet, the way station would offer up both pools. Our performing arts troupe was eligible for these same special privileges.

As our group of girl soldiers entered the women's bathing area, we saw a bare-chested man working in the pool. He was huge and rough-hewn, with a jaw so large it dragged down to his breastbone. When he spotted us, he became flustered and hurriedly tried to unroll his rolled-up pants legs, causing them to drag in the water. He'd been sent to clear the sulphur stains off the bottom of the pool. The residue had built up in successive layers, and the colors had become intermingled, forming patterns like those of cloisonné enamels or the three-color drip glazes on Tang dynasty ceramics.

We had noticed a gathering of Tibetans in a nearby meadow, and we asked the man what they were doing. First he was startled and looked all around until he was certain that we were addressing him.

"Ba- Ba- Bath Festival," he stammered in Gansu dialect. His face was so dark it was almost greenish—a distinct contrast to the Tibetans' swarthiness, which is closer to violet. His teeth were the color of tea, his gums pink. He picked up a green army overcoat tattered beyond repair that had been lying next to the pool, put it on and relinquished the bathing area to us.

By the time we left the bathing area, it was high noon, and the air temperature had risen by ten degrees centigrade up to twenty degrees. We were passing behind the spa when someone yelled, "Oh, my God!" We looked over and saw a cloud of steam; in it was a milling crowd of dark violet male and female bodies.

They were all descending into a makeshift ditch. The water stank.

Its surface was coated with a film from our morning bath that stuck to the water like a skin on boiled milk. The whole ditch filled with people, men and women together, protruding from the water like seedlings in a rice patty.

Before the military had taken over the hot springs and divided them into separate areas for men and women, the springs had belonged to them. Back then, they had ample space in which to bathe, and they didn't have to soak in someone else's run-off.

"Hey, what are we looking at?" one of us remarked suddenly.

We were about to run away, out of both fear and excitement, when suddenly we saw the beautiful blind woman, standing off at a distance. She had partially bared her shoulders but left her breasts well covered, exposing nothing but allowing one to imagine everything. The half-shoulders protruding from her robe were delicate and slender. Inclining her body toward the sound, she was "looking" eagerly into the ditch. She had spread an apron on the ground to display her little red apples. One by one, she picked up each apple, licked it all the way around, then polished it with her robe. Soon the apples were all gleaming brightly.

When evening came and we set up the stage, we were all still giggling. Our eyes had really stolen quite a sight. The way station's discipline on this matter was very strict: no one was allowed to go behind the hot springs during the Bath Festival, and anyone who looked on would be held responsible for the consequences. The Tibetans would have a wild time among themselves, but if a soldier stood by and watched, they would stop their celebration and protest.

The way station had spared no effort in trying to get along with the Tibetans. In other locales, the Han Chinese oppression had given the Tibetans cause to revolt, and this isolated place had felt the repercussions. Even in peaceful times, the Tibetans, who were the way station's only source of fresh meat, would bring beef and mutton that had started to turn and proffer it to the way station as a gift. If the way station had prepared any steamed bread with too much or too little sourdough, it would give this to the Tibetans in return.

Before putting on our theatrical makeup, we washed our faces, and the man from Gansu made five or six trips with his shoulder pole and buckets to bring us hot water. As he squatted down to roll a cigarette, a soldier walked over and planted a kick on his buttocks. He didn't react. Some other soldiers passing by grabbed his old army cap with its limp brim and pulled it askew, covering half his face. He just kept on smoking. Finally the lieutenant on duty strode up, prominently wearing the red armband of his office. He crooked his index finger at the man, as if calling a dog. The man from Gansu stood up at once, bowing repeatedly from the waist, his two long arms dangling on both sides. "Hey, you big lunk, what are you looking at there?" the lieutenant demanded, shooting a sidelong glance at a group of girl soldiers applying rouge. "Haven't you seen enough of that stuff before?!" None of us understood what he was talking about. "Don't just stand there," the lieutenant bellowed. "Go fetch more water!"

With a snort of disgust the lieutenant cleared his face of all expression. Trying to defuse the tension, we told him we had more than enough water. The lieutenant forced a smile and replied, "What else is he good for? Let him go!"

The man from Gansu heaved his carrying pole onto his muscular shoulders and stumbled off, the ground shaking in his wake. The lieutenant stared at the vanishing silhouette of his back and muttered, "That son of a bitch!"

"How can such an old man still be a soldier?" one of us asked. "Who's a soldier? Him? A soldier?" the lieutenant gestured toward the now distant figure. Then the lieutenant told us the man's story. He had come to Tibet as a soldier when the army was suppressing an uprising. Back then, the two hot springs lay supine out in the open air. When the Bath Festival rolled around, the Tibetans, both men and women, were playing about and splashing in the water. One day the man from Gansu happened by and stood watching as if addicted. The Tibetans seized him and were about to beat him to death. Soldiers from the way station intervened and demanded he be released to their custody. The military resolved the matter by transferring him back to Gansu Province that winter.

But the next year he returned. All that was left of him was a huge rack of skin and bones. Many people in his village had starved, and everyone in his family had died except him. The way station did not drive him out after that. He picked up others' discarded rags to wear, fished out leftovers from the bottoms of the cooking pots and did odd jobs that no one else wanted to do.

The next day before our evening performance, we went to Yajiang City to see the sights. On the way, we saw the blind Tibetan woman and the man from Gansu. The man was carrying his shoulder pole, the pails on each side brimming with red apples. The blind woman walked behind him, empty-handed except for the hem of his tattered army overcoat, which she clutched as she trailed along. His strides were large, hers small. No matter how they tried, they just couldn't find a common rhythm. The pair didn't speak. Their conversation was an alternating exchange of laughter, a completely silly kind of laughter. The blind woman's head was covered with flowers, so densely arranged that they looked like the dandelion crown worn by the female general Mu Guiying in Chinese opera. The man from Gansu had a ball of flowers dangling about his chest. On the high plains, all of the wildflowers have short stems. You can't make them into a bouquet; you can only tie them together into a ball.

That night after our performance, we girls conspired to bathe in the hot springs again. We were about to leave the Yajiang area, and there was no telling when we would be able to bathe again. Walking along toward the springs, we trod as lightly as thieves, afraid the leadership would stop us. The leaders only allowed one bath per visit, even for dignitaries. We also feared the Tibetans. The leaders had taught us not to look down on the Tibetans, but they had also told us that Tibetans would sometimes capture a female soldier, put her in a big leather bag, carry her away to some far-off mountain gorge and use her to breed little female soldiers.

The hot springs lay in a basin, which was hidden until you started up the mountain slope. Once you got to the top of the slope, it was as plain as the nose on your face. It was close to midnight, yet the twilight had still not faded. For hours there was this red and gold sunset hanging in the clouds like an open festering wound. Where did that big flock of crows go during the day? And where did those fiendishly happy Tibetan people go all day?

One of us whispered softly, "The sky looks like People's Road." Hearing her refer again to the main street of Chengdu, Sichuan Province's capital, the rest of us laughed. "You compare every pretty sight to People's Road," someone said, "because all you know is People's Road."

"All right," she replied. "So I'm from a little village in Sichuan. But at least I know People's Road—but what does that big weird guy from Gansu know?"

Another girl shot back in agreement: "He's so big! He's disgusting!"

"Somebody at the way station said that one time they got a shipment of tangerines," the first girl continued. "He ate them, skin and all. They were so bitter he was miserable. Nobody told him you had to peel them before you ate them. They all peeled their own behind his back. One by one, he gave all his tangerines away. He couldn't take it any more, eating them with the skin on."

We had not yet completed our descent into the basin when we suddenly stood motionless. Usually one of us would let out a piercing scream at a critical moment like this. Fortunately, no one cried out.

The sky held the final embers of twilight. The blind woman was standing naked in the ditch that caught the hot springs' run-off, slowly rubbing the water upward along her body with both hands. She didn't know how murky and dirty the water was. Most of the flowers in her hair had fallen out helter-skelter, leaving just a few in inappropriate places. Her hips were slender and lean above the water, which came up to the top of her thighs. Repeatedly, she bent her knees, brought her cupped hands over her head and poured water onto her body. This utterly repetitive motion made us feel as if she were immobile. She was completely calm, totally passive.

If this scene had consisted only of her, no one would have paid much attention. What was jarring was the presence of the man from

Gansu. He was so huge as he squatted there, or perhaps he knelt, staring, his enormous jaw hanging down loosely. Though he was absolutely still, one felt movement in his motionless form, and this invisible movement contorted his stillness.

None of us reported the incident. We all carried off an uneasy feeling into our sleep. Toward morning, there was a commotion throughout the way station. We heard they were looking for someone. Looking for him.

Our performing arts troupe joined in the search. The Tibetans had been paying attention to the fraternization between the man from Gansu and the blind woman for some time now. The previous night, they had all come out and protested. Naturally, the man from Gansu ran to the way station, but they wouldn't let him to hide there for fear the Tibetans would level the place. So he ran off. The Tibetans were invited into the station, and the officers helped them search for him in order to show them that he did not belong to the way station.

When the search party entered a nearby woods, they startled a colony of crows, turning the sky from clear to mottled in an instant. When they finally captured him that afternoon, both his legs had been wounded by the Tibetans' spears. His tattered green army pants were soaked red, and his stocky legs dangled uselessly from loss of blood. They dragged him back to the station, a Tibetan and a soldier supporting him, one on each side. He was not severely wounded, but he appeared not to have understood what had happened.

We were stunned to see so many Tibetans gather here so quickly. It was as if they had just sprung out of the ground. One could never understand all of this place's hidden perils. The day was extremely hot. Flocks of crows, cawing, rose up into the sky like bursts of fireworks.

The man from Gansu was shoved into the vast courtyard of the way station. Amidst the crowd, even the beautiful blind woman stared at the large bleeding body pushed into the middle of the yard. She was still carrying her red apples, red to the point of saturation.

The soldiers and the Tibetans finally reached an agreement: they would tie him up and send him to district headquarters. But he was too heavy to be carried on a stretcher. A truck stood by, its engine running, waiting impatiently. The man from Gansu raised his head; he appeared to be ashamed of all the trouble his hulking body was causing everyone. When they stuffed him into the truck he groaned out the word "thirsty" a few times. Everyone pretended not to hear.

The next morning, our performance troupe set out again. Everyone in the truck was listless. The soldiers at the way station had also been somber, something nagging at them, depressed about something.

When we crossed over the mountain, it started snowing. By now we were accustomed to seeing it snow here in June, so no one said a word. When we rounded a bend, she was there again. The truck slowed down, the driver waiting for our instructions. We remained as silent as a load of cargo.

The woman approached a few steps, but the truck lurched forward from her touch, spinning her and grazing her shoulder. Leaping into the empty space where the truck had been, the woman fell face-forward onto the road, spilling her red apples on the snow-covered ground, so red they looked filthy, as if a festering ulcer had formed on the snow.

Notes to "Red Apples"

Page 115 **Gansu Province:** a desolate region of mountains and desert located in Northwest China.

Page 118 **"All that was left of him was a huge rack of skin and bones":** in the aftermath of the Great Leap Forward, when villages had been forced to neglect agriculture in favor of small-scale industry, China experienced a great famine in which millions of people died.

Page 118 **"It was close to midnight, yet the twilight had still not faded":** all of China is on Beijing time. In Tibet, thousands of kilometers west of Beijing, people get up in the middle of the night to go to school or work, and the sun sets very late according to "clock time."

無
非
男
女

Nothing More than Male and Female

Yuchuan was from another province, so when she arrived in the city, she could only live with Cai Yao's family. After three days, Yuchuan had already determined that this was by no means your typical family with the mother-in-law whispering to the daughter-in-law, the younger sister chasing off the elder brother's wife and the unmarried daughters all vying with each other in beauty. Even though Cai Yao doted on Yuchuan, whenever Father was lecturing at the dinner table he would murmur in agreement, cutting off Yuchuan's interjections. By the fourth day, Yuchuan had still not met Cai Yao's younger brother. From seven to eleven in the morning, before everyone went to work, left the house, or sat down to write or knit, they would all periodically run over to a door next to the bathroom and call out twice: "Lao Wu! Lao Wu!" The way they called out seemed anxious, as if calling out to check if Lao Wu were still alive. Saturday morning, Yuchuan decided not to go out. Cai Yao had already taken her to see all the obligatory sights, and she wanted to stay at home and collect herself before starting her new job. As soon as Spring Festival was over, she would go to the hospital's personnel department to register. Perhaps they would assign her to the outpatient clinic. Nursing school graduates were generally assigned there first to break them in.

"Well, all right then, I'll go to work today," Cai Yao said, searching all his pockets for his bicycle key. He was an editor at a publishing house, but it seemed as if he went to work only when he had nothing better to do. His major asset was a reliable source of manuscripts. All the region's literary lions were rounded up in the rabbit-hutch-like building where he lived.

After Cai Yao had gotten dressed, he thought of something and walked back into the apartment, hollering "Lao Wu, Lao Wu!" The door to Lao Wu's room was so narrow, it didn't seem like anyone could possibly sleep in there. The first time it was pointed out to her as Lao Wu's room, Yuchuan was taken aback: "Aiya, that room looks like a storage closet!"

"What do you mean that 'room.' That *is* a storage closet!" younger sister Xiaopin replied. Yuchuan and Xiaopin shared a room together in the Cai household. Xiaopin was working as a teaching assistant at the university and generally left the house around ten a.m. She would call out "Lao Wu!" at precisely 9:50 a.m.

The first few days, Yuchuan was exhausted from sightseeing and would go to bed not long after dinner. Once she woke up in the middle of the night and heard Xiaopin arguing with someone in a low voice: "Let me use the bathroom first! If you go in first, I'm gonna die waiting!" After a while, Xiaopin tiptoed across the bedroom to the mirror and plucked the hairpins out of her hair. Yuchuan asked her who she had been talking to just now. Xiaopin climbed under the down comforter in the other bed and replied, "Lao Wu, of course! Who else?"

The next day, by the time Father had finished his morning four hours of writing and had called out "Lao Wu," he was the last in the family to do so, and Mother was already in the kitchen preparing the midday meal.

Yuchuan felt a bit flustered by the strangeness of it all—everyone waiting for this Lao Wu, whom she had never seen, to emerge. There was no response at all. Father went into the kitchen to inspect the quality of the noon meal. Yuchuan was sitting on the rug, rummaging through a pile of magazines and idly flipping through one of them, when some sensation made her look up. She saw a delicate thin young man standing in the doorway. She knew who he was but could not demonstratively call out "Lao Wu." His hair was long and curly, and twenty percent of it was white. His forehead was large and broad, but the accompanying cheeks inclined precipitously. This, in addition to a small, slightly pursed mouth, gave him a bit of a feminine appearance. He bore not the slightest resemblance to the image Yuchuan had developed of this "Lao Wu" the whole family had been hollering at.

He walked in and smiled briefly at Yuchuan. He bent his waist to examine the open magazine Yuchuan was now holding to one side and frowned slightly. He focused his eyes and thought a moment, drew the issue in Yuchuan's hand toward himself to have a look, then said, "Oh, now the order's all messed up!"

Yuchuan immediately put down the magazine in her hand and said, "I didn't take them anywhere else."

His fingers fleetingly rearranged the pile of magazines. He didn't speak. His whole person, in addition to having a smell of toothpaste, carried a rather unusual odor. Yuchuan knew it was a medicinal smell. He wore a dark blue cotton shirt. His shoulders were not as broad as Cai Yao's, nor was his neck as thick, and when he twisted his head, you could see the tendons bulge out in a frightful way. Cai Yao had always spoken about his sister Xiaopin, about how intelligent she was, how erudite, and how hard it was to marry her off. When it came to his younger brother, he had only one phrase: "He's such a bother!"

"Are you going out?" Mother asked, standing in the living room wrapped in a large apron.

"No." Yuchuan discovered that she and Lao Wu had answered in unison. She looked at him, and he at her.

"So are you having lunch with us?"

This time Yuchuan understood that it was not she who was being asked, so she stood up and prepared to help set the table. This family was not of the usual "don't get up, you're a guest" and "eat, eat, all this food here is not an offering for the ancestors" variety. They were not as punctilious toward many things as other households.

"No. I have milk."

As the three of them sat down at the table, Yuchuan saw Lao Wu scoop up the magazines and go into his pantrylike room. Then she heard a hasty rustling from inside. Yuchuan had asked Cai Yao, how can Lao Wu draw a breath in there? Cai Yao had answered, didn't you see the wooden slat blinds he's rigged up over his door? He's keeping himself like a cricket.

"Was it Xiaopin who brought his things into the living room?" Mother asked in a low voice.

"How should I know?" Father answered, not bothering to lower his voice.

"If it wasn't Xiaopin, then it was Da Mao," Mother said. Da Mao was Cai Yao's childhood nickname.

Yuchuan, uneasy, said she had just been leafing through the magazines.

Mother replied hastily, "It's all right. Lao Wu is writing a book about petroglyphs. He's been collecting those magazines for a long time. Da Mao and Xiaopin are very bad — whenever they go into Lao Wu's room, they mess up his things."

"Oh, so it's possible to make Lao Wu's room messier than it already is?" Father said, straining to suppress a laugh. Finally he did laugh out loud.

Yuchuan looked first toward Mother, then toward Father, not at all sure that she had understood them. Then there was the sound of a door opening, and Lao Wu came out. He looked at the three of them seated at the table, then turned toward the refrigerator at the edge of the dining area, took out a bottle of milk and an egg and walked into the kitchen. Mother rested her chopsticks on the edge of her bowl and listened to the sounds coming from the kitchen. After a while, there came a "ch-rrr" sound. Mother called out.

"Lao Wu, you were watching the pot and still made the milk boil over?"

No sound came in reply. When Lao Wu came out holding his bowl in front of him, Mother craned her neck to look. "After boiling over, there's only half a bowl left? Will you have enough to eat?" "Why do you ask so many questions?" Father asked Mother, his face still wearing a smile.

Lao Wu slowly walked back to his room, his waist tilted slightly backward. Yuchuan realized for the first time that Lao Wu's midsection was somewhat caved in, making him seem shorter than he really was.

In the evening, Yuchuan went out to meet Cai Yao coming home from work, intercepting him two blocks away from the apartment building. When she saw him, she said with excitement and agitation on her face, "I met Lao Wu today!"

"Did you meet Lao Wu today, or did you meet a tiger on the way?" Cai Yao rhymed playfully. Cai Yao was not tall, sort of like a truncated column. Yuchuan was nine years younger than he. Cai Yao always joked that she was "twenty-three, still growing like a tree." After she was fully grown, we would see which of the two of them would wear high heels, he joked.

When they arrived at the courtyard of their apartment building and saw some neighbors, Cai Yao introduced Yuchuan as "my girlfriend." As they walked inside the building, Yuchuan asked him what he liked most about her. He didn't hesitate for a moment: "You're pretty!" While they were walking upstairs, they ran into Lao Wu coming downstairs. Lao Wu was wearing a maroon stocking cap, and the cap had pressed some of his hair to each side of his eyebrows, making him look even more like a girl. Seeing the two of them, he raised his eyes slightly, his eyelids revealing two deep folds as if he were fatigued or emaciated.

"Where are you going, Lao Wu?" Cai Yao asked.

"Going out for a while."

"Are you still doing your paintings?"

"Just going out."

"Got any money with you?"

"I've already eaten."

Yuchuan thought this an odd exchange for two brothers.

Lao Wu raised his eyes toward Yuchuan's face. Yuchuan wanted to answer with a smile, but it was already too late. He had already averted his gaze.

After making sure that Lao Wu was far off, Yuchuan asked, "You're Da Mao, the eldest, and Xiaopin is the second child, so how did he get to be Lao Wu, the fifth child?"

"It's a long story." Cai Yao took out his key, opened the door and said quietly, "I'll tell you some other time, otherwise if my mother hears, there'll be trouble." Inside the apartment, they found a note on the refrigerator door from his father, informing them that Father and Mother had been invited out to dinner. Xiaopin wasn't home either. Yuchuan immediately pleaded with Cai Yao to hear the mystery of Lao Wu.

Cai Yao paid her no heed. He took off his cotton quilted jacket and draped it over his arm, then checked each room. After confirming that, indeed, no one was home, he rushed over to her and embraced her eagerly. Yuchuan knew he could not endure much longer. Her face dodged his kisses with their scent of cigarette smoke. Cai Yao pushed Yuchuan into Lao Wu's room and pinned her down on a bed not more than three feet wide. The ceiling was hung with many gourds, large and small, carved with many rough designs and smoked to create a deeper bas-relief effect. When Yuchuan was laid flat on the bed, her eyes followed a rubber tube next to her. Suddenly she realized what must cause the medicinal smell of this bed and of Lao Wu's body.

"This is Lao Wu's room!" Yuchuan started to struggle.

"Don't move!" Cai Yao said. "This is the safest place. If someone comes, they won't come in here first."

"But what if Lao Wu comes back?"

"Him? He doesn't matter! Anyway, he wouldn't think of this."

"Why not?"

"Don't get distracted, okay?"

An hour later, when the two of them had come to rest, Cai Yao pulled the down comforter over Yuchuan. Even the comforter had a medicinal smell, as well as a sort of not-so-fresh feeling about it.

"Now tell me!" she egged him on.

"When Lao Wu was very small, he had some kind of disease that caused both his kidneys to fail. The doctor said he wouldn't live to be thirty, and he couldn't get married. My mother has never been superstitious, but she became superstitious then. When she heard all this about Lao Wu, she went to our ancestral graveyard and made two false graves. She said she did it to fool the King of the Netherworld, as if to say, 'O King of the Dead, you've already carried off our third child and fourth child, please leave this fifth child to us.' That's how my little brother came to be called Lao Wu, Fifth Child."

"Has he known since childhood that he wouldn't live long?"

"I'm not sure when he found out. When all the young people were sent down to the countryside, he was at the very tail end. His illness should have kept him in the city, but at that time my father had been slapped with all the bad labels—counter-revolutionary author, undercover spy—so they sent Lao Wu down to the farm anyway, although the duties he got were a bit better than working in the rice paddies. My younger brother just hated to hear people say he was useless or handicapped, so he kept up his work pace. That was when his illness got much worse. My mother went around pleading with everyone until they finally give him a medical discharge. I spent the whole night bicycling to his village and then hauled him back eighty kilometers on my bike. He was so weak he couldn't sit up. I got a rope and tied us both together, back to back. Once we were back, he spent more time in the hospital than at home, and a lot of it in the critical care unit. It was around that time, when it was my turn to keep the night vigil, that I read his diary. Ever since he was little, the whole family had to guess what was on his mind. Maybe all people with weak constitutions become introverted. Back then, I found a diary under his pillow, and I thought, it won't be long before this is no longer a secret anyway. If we knew what he was thinking before then, maybe we could do something to ease the situation a bit. I never anticipated that he would be so very perceptive, objective and rational toward himself. There was one page where he wrote that before he was thirty, there were certain things he wanted to accomplish. Even now, I still remember them as clearly as when I first read them: he wanted to travel ten thousand kilometers, write a book, plant a hundred trees, put on a solo exhibition of his paintings, fly once in an airplane and fall in love once."

"So, then," Yuchuan pressed Cai Yao's hand which was stroking her waist, "in his own mind, he had already counted everything out?"

"Yes. Otherwise, how could he become more and more idiosyncratic? My father found him a job as a proofreader at a publishing house. A month later, when he found out Lao Wu wasn't going to his job any more, my father asked him what was the matter. He said he had already quit because that job was 'sitting, eating and waiting to die.' My father got upset and said that *not* going to work was sitting, eating and waiting to die. Lao Wu shot back that he would not sit and eat anything that belonged to Father and Mother, and he would not die in this house. Since then, if he eats in this house, he puts fifty *fen* on the table. Nobody knows where he earns that money.

"Does he have a girlfriend?"

"A girlfriend? What girl would want to get involved in something that has a head but no tail? You'd have to fool somebody, and that would be dishonest. Actually, Lao Wu is very attractive to women, but he tells it like it is. Women are all very practical. Who wouldn't be afraid to spend half her life waiting hand and foot on someone? If he dies, then that's that, and if he doesn't die, who could bear hovering around a sickbed until he does? Whenever he eats, sleeps or goes to the bathroom, our whole family worries."

Yuchuan inclined her face to look at the catheter by the bed and was astonished that anyone in this world could suffer so much in silence and still be able to carry on. When Cai Yao's desire returned, she was staring at the gourds on the ceiling. Without knowing she'd been counting, she had discovered that there were twenty-eight of them.

"Is Lao Wu twenty-eight?"

In the midst of his arousal, Cai Yao stopped for a moment and asked, "How did you know?" Yuchuan could hear his annoyance and vexation.

At that moment, someone came home. It wasn't Xiaopin. The first thing Xiaopin would do is put on some music.

"Never mind. It's just Lao Wu," Cai Yao said, panting.

The door to the room, bolted from the inside, was pulled from the outside a few times, sending flashes of light through the cracks.

"Sorry Lao Wu. Wait in another room for a while, okay?"

"Why aren't you in your *own* room . . . ?" Lao Wu asked ruefully.

"Quit talking nonsense," Cai Yao said, jumping up and getting dressed and rattling his metal belt buckle for all to hear. While he was picking up Yuchuan's clothing and accessories and tossing them to her, he leaned toward the door and called out, "Can't you stay in my room?!" Cai Yao's room adjoined the kitchen, and the door separating it was made of glass. Yuchuan once heard Father discussing in a low voice: if Da Mao gets married and he hasn't been able to get his own place yet, we'll seal off that door, or at least replace it with a soundproof wooden door.

Yuchuan followed Cai Yao out the door, wishing she could disappear. She knew she had a terribly flushed face and disheveled hair. The next day, Lao Wu put a butterfly-shaped hair clip on the newspaper she was reading.

Yuchuan looked up.

"Yours. I found it on my bed," Lao Wu said.

Yuchuan thought it might be appropriate to say thank you, yet at the same time saying anything might seem too brazen. She felt her thick eyelashes grow heavy, so heavy that her eyelids could not support them, and they began to quiver. She looked at Lao Wu, expecting him to leave quickly, yet he did not; rather he drummed with two fingers on the desk where she was sitting.

"This doesn't look good," Lao Wu said.

"What?" Yuchuan replied, shocked.

Lao Wu pointed to the hair clip. "This." He smiled both harshly and with embarrassment. "It's so *ordinary.*"

Yuchuan didn't know what to say.

She felt Lao Wu looking at her. Many people said she had an elegant profile. She turned her face. His eyes had already wandered off to the television, yet Yuchuan felt his gaze was really still where it had been, still on her left profile.

At that moment, Mother came in and exclaimed, "Lao Wu, I asked you to buy soft tofu. How did you end up buying dried tofu? Why do you need to stand in line half a day just to buy dried tofu?"

Father interrupted: "So what are *you* doing?"

"What am *I* doing? If I were to stand in all the lines, who would do the cooking around here? With dried tofu, I can't make you all a proper *ma-po* tofu.

"Then make *dried ma-po* tofu!" Father replied. "What do you expect from Lao Wu? All he knows how to do is boil milk for himself."

Lao Wu acted as if he hadn't heard.

Later, Lao Wu finished his dinner of boiled milk and an egg before everyone else, then with an obvious, exaggerated gesture, he pressed fifty *fen* on the table. Father looked at that money, stretched his chopsticks out halfway, then suddenly stopped short and yelled, "Out! Get the hell out of here!"

Lao Wu turned and walked slowly toward the doorway, his waist still tilted, and took his overcoat and stocking cap off the coat rack. Half murmuring and half yelling, Xiaopin called out in a low voice, "Lao Wu . . ." She turned toward Father and said, "Dad, if you talk that way to Lao Wu, I'll get the hell out of here along with him! So we've lost out on a meal of *ma-po* tofu. Do you want to lose him, too, with such talk? At least he knows how to boil milk, but you've never even done that by yourself. Mom has always waited on you hand and foot!"

Mother's tears rolled down. She sobbed and said, "None of you ever gives the other any quarter. Yuchuan hasn't even come into our family yet, and already we're scaring her off." Cai Yao didn't make a sound. He grinned at Yuchuan and made gestures toward his ears to indicate that she should let all this go in one ear and out the other. "Dad always talks about Lao Wu's boiled milk," Xiaopin said, more softly but still with pique. "But Dad must know that Lao Wu drinks milk all the time, and it simply can't be helped!"

Yuchuan discovered that, even though Xiaopin defended Lao Wu this time, every Sunday when she cooked, she would always yell, "Lao Wu, just to boil a mouthful of milk and an egg you have to take up two burners and cause me all this trouble?. . . Can't you wait until I've finished cooking dinner?"

Some weeks later, when she came home from work, Yuchuan found a thermos bottle from the children's school days. She boiled milk for Lao Wu and poured it into the thermos. Lao Wu blinked his eyes as he saw how easily she took care of the whole matter. Yuchuan raised her head and smiled toward him playfully as if to say, "Aren't I smart?" They were the only ones in the kitchen.

They were the only ones in the whole apartment. Father and mother had gone to Beidaihe to escape the heat. Xiaopin had protested her father's treatment of Lao Wu by going to stay at the house of one of her friends from work, though this gesture was gradually losing its point. Cai Yao had gone off to collect an author's manuscript, taking an afternoon train to a small city several hundred kilometers away where the author lived, and canceling the plans he'd made with Yuchuan to see a movie. He said many other publishing houses were vying with each other for this author's works, so he had to take drastic pre-emptive action.

"You want to go see a movie?" Yuchuan asked. "I've got two tickets. Your brother is off on some urgent business, so I've got an extra one. It's a new film."

"No, thank you. All those movies are so tacky."

"But you're not doing anything anyway."

"Yes, I am. I'm so busy I don't know where to begin."

"Anything I can help with?" She gave a tight smile, meaning that there was no need for him to pretend.

He shook his head.

"What are you up to? Perhaps it's something I happen to know something about."

Lao Wu said matter-of-factly, "I have to forge two marriage certificates. Two friends of mine want to arrange abortions, and without a marriage certificate, the hospital won't stop asking questions."

"Do you know how?" She carefully avoided using the word "forge."

"I do it all the time. They're going to pay me."

Yuchuan thought to herself that she was now the only person in the household who knew the source of Lao Wu's income. At the beginning of spring, she and some of her nurse co-workers had gone to the free market. While there, they'd seen some foreigners in a semicircle looking at something. Through the oscillating web of people, she saw a delicate human figure with his back bent over like a bow. Her co-workers wanted to crowd in, but she backed away because she saw clearly that it was Lao Wu.

She had also seen clearly that he was hunched over a short folding card table demonstrating the art of cutting stone chops, displaying his artistry. Yuchuan could never bear to see people performing for a crowd, especially if the one on display was a graying Lao Wu who already knew his own destiny.

Once Yuchuan saw that Lao Wu had scalded himself so badly while drinking his boiled milk that he stuck out his tongue and crooked his neck. She walked over to him and stroked his back. She didn't know why she did that, or why Lao Wu's underground activities did not cause her revulsion but instead awakened her sympathetic impulses.

Actually, Lao Wu required no sympathy. He stood in the kitchen and described calmly and seriously the process of forging a document, how to go to the print shop and find lead type and how to crunch them into a metal plate until a seal-stamper was created. Yuchuan rested her chin on both fists as she watched Lao Wu's gesturing hands. The time he turned over the magazine before her face, she had secretly been as surprised by his long, fine and soft hand as by his uncharacteristic invasiveness. His hand was a not-too-fresh, even stale white. Perhaps a hand that constantly did illicit things in dark places should manifest this form and color.

Yuchuan had no intention of going to see the movie by herself. With the TV turned on, she read a novel on the sofa but soon fell asleep. She awakened to find her neck covered with sweat. Lao Wu had not yet returned. Immediately she thought, if Lao Wu has or hasn't returned, what concern is that of mine? Why so anxious about his return? She wasn't sure if it was loneliness or worry that made her wait up like this with her heart fluttering.

Actually, Lao Wu's presence caused everyone in the family to feel an unnamed loneliness. No matter how lively things were, if Lao Wu appeared on the scene, that loneliness reappeared, infecting the entire atmosphere around him. His loneliness was terribly contagious. So she concluded she could not be waiting up for Lao Wu's return to relieve her loneliness, if indeed that was what she was feeling. Much less could it be out of worry. Lao Wu nearly always returned home around 3:00 AM. It was said that he borrowed a friend's studio to paint in, and the studio was only unoccupied at night. No one in the family had ever worried about him. As weak as he was, he was still a man over six feet tall.

After twelve, Yuchuan took a cool shower. After she got out of the shower, she heard the sound of a key clattering in the lock, and she almost shouted for joy, "Lao Wu, you're back!" She was so happy, so effusive. This feeling had only occurred before in her childhood when she had been quarantined for hepatitis and her parents had come to visit her.

"Haven't you gone to sleep yet?" Lao Wu asked.

"It's too hot! Aren't you hot?" Lao Wu's slightly enlarged eyeballs made Yuchuan aware of her unusual behavior.

"Not too bad." Lao Wu's T-shirt was hoisted up to his chest, exposing his lower torso. At that moment, he quickly rolled it down. Once when Yuchuan came home from work, Lao Wu was barechested, helping Xiaopin nail up her mosquito net. When he saw Yuchuan, he quickly ran to his room. When he came out again, he was wearing a T-shirt as wrinkled as pickled cabbage.

"Not too bad?! I took five showers today!" Yuchuan said. Her filmy pink silk nightgown, caught by the breeze of the electric fan, fluttered here and flattened there, outlining her body from every angle.

Lao Wu walked over to turn on the television and flipped through the stations without coming up with anything. Yuchuan laughed.

"Lao Wu, since when are there any programs on after midnight? If you don't want to talk with me, I can certainly leave!" She knew that her directness would make him nervous. In reality, it was the phenomenon of the two of them being the only ones left in the house that made him nervous. Lao Wu smiled somewhat shyly, but his eyebrows were still frowning slightly in annoyance. This expression made him extremely good-looking, extremely uncommon, Yuchuan thought. Lao Wu asked perfunctorily about the movie. Yuchuan said she had given the tickets to the neighbors. She didn't want him to think that she lacked good taste. Lao Wu thought of something and pulled a small object out of his pocket. It was a fish carved out of hardwood with a rustic look to it, except it had a little less crudeness and a little more artifice. It was a highly original piece. Lao Wu turned it over, and Yuchuan discovered it was a hair clip.

"Do you want it?"

Delighted, Yuchuan replied, "Yeah!"

"I made it and asked a friend to help me sell it. But it's too hard to sell off."

"Why? It's so pretty!"

"My price was too high."

"Then why didn't you sell it cheaper?"

"If they want something cheap, why buy mine?"

Yuchuan took the hair clip over to the full-length mirror in the foyer to try it on. Her hair was too thick, and she couldn't shut the clip. Lao Wu said he would adjust it. Yuchuan kept on fiddling with it. This time as she pulled in her chin and put both her arms behind her head, Yuchuan caught sight of her two armpits very lightly covered with downy hair. Then she saw Lao Wu in the mirror, his lips pursed with some effort, his sensitive, or perhaps melancholy, eyebrow casting a sliver of dark shadow above his eyes. Suddenly she realized that much more was revealed than just her two armpits. She suddenly dropped her arms to her sides, giving a pretext: "My arms are so sore!"

Lao Wu said he had to see just how tight or how loose he needed to adjust the clip. He took a pinch of her long hair and timidly arranged it into the clip. She angled her body slightly, still staring from the corner of her eye into the mirror. The contrast between Lao Wu's unearthly white hands and Yuchuan's vibrant black hair was so stark it was jarring. Lao Wu also comprehended the marvel of this contrast and slowed his hand movements, finally bringing them to a standstill. Yuchuan saw his two eyes raise two lines of even deeper eye-folds, as if expending effort, trying to see through something.

Yuchuan turned abruptly and said, "I'm going to bed now," and walked into her room. As she started to close the bedroom door, she hesitated. Should she turn the bolt or shouldn't she? The door bolt was to prevent people from barging in: was there any need to use it with Lao Wu? If she didn't bolt it, would it appear as if she were exercising too little propriety? Suddenly the night became oddly still—almost malevolently so—as if listening for whether or not she bolted the door. Either way her decision would be heard in that stillness. Would be heard by Lao Wu. The door would make a "ka-chak" sound that would prick the ears harshly. It would needlessly reaffirm and emphasize the moral line that was not to be transgressed. Her hands poised awkwardly on the door bolt. Then, led by her intuition, she opened the door with a "wha" sound.

Lao Wu, for no apparent reason, was standing in the doorway only three paces away from her. He looked at her as if fearful, the half-filled milk glass in his hand angling dangerously.

"Hey, Lao Wu, it's so hot—think I'll sleep with the door open. Let the air circulate, get a little breeze." Yuchuan thought her voice sounded very natural and aboveboard. "How about you? There are so many empty rooms, why sleep in that stuffy little cupboard of yours?"

"I don't mind the heat. I'm used to it. I have an electric fan."

Yuchuan saw Lao Wu drink his milk and carry the glass over to the kitchen sink, leaving only an empty clouded glass. That night her emotions were rattled. She didn't know if it was because she hadn't locked the door, or because Lao Wu finally went to sleep in his coffin-like room, bolting the door behind him with a "ka-chak" sound.

The next day was a Sunday. First thing in the morning, she received a long-distance call from Cai Yao saying that by hook or by crook he had to get that manuscript and make sure that no one else would intercept it.

"How much longer are you going to stay there?"

"A week. Ten days at the most." At his end, Cai Yao could hear her discontent.

"No! I want you to come back *right now!* Immediately!"

"Be a little reasonable, all right? This is my *work!* If I make good connections for work, I can be promoted to deputy editor-in-chief. We can get an apartment assigned to us at the end of the year and get married!"

"Come back this minute! Get on the train right now!"

Cai Yao couldn't see her and so didn't know she was stamping her feet, holding back her tears, struck by some sort of fear. He didn't understand her loss of composure and used his utmost skill to coax her, saying he would take her to get that dress she had looked at ten times but could never bring herself to buy.

For several days now she hadn't seen Lao Wu. She didn't know whether, intentionally or unintentionally, she was avoiding him or being avoided by him. Every day before going to work, she still boiled milk and poured it into the thermos bottle. One day after dark when she came back from work, she saw Lao Wu carefully slicing fresh ginger. When she asked him why he was slicing so much fresh ginger, he replied that he wanted to fry an egg. She laughed hard. "Why do you want to use fresh ginger to fry an egg?"

"You mean I shouldn't?" he asked, watching her laugh.

At that moment, Xiaopin arrived carrying some groceries. Xiaopin told Lao Wu to forget about his egg and join them for dinner. She and Yuchuan talked as they cooked. After the three of them had finished eating happily and peacefully, Xiaopin suddenly said, "Lao Wu, if you pull out those fifty *fen,* then I don't know you any more! If you really insist on paying, then pay more. Nowadays all the prices have gone up. Fifty *fen,* to buy a whole meal!"

Yuchuan didn't dare look up at Lao Wu, guessing that he must be very distressed. In fact, he wasn't. Lao Wu smiled with ease and equanimity. After Xiaopin had gotten out all she had wanted to say, Lao Wu said very slowly, "Well, you sure talk like you *used* to know me."

"Ah-yo! Don't be such a complete cipher all the time. You're so hard to know!" Xiaopin hugged her own shoulders and leaned against the back of her chair.

Yuchuan, anxious to change the atmosphere, interrupted by entreating Xiaopin to move back home. Xiaopin replied that her girl-friend's place was close to school, and she was spared the need to take a stinky crowded bus every day. Moreover, she didn't have to look constantly at her parents' faces filled with worry that they wouldn't be able to marry her off. If she lived at home, she would have to listen to their discourses on marriage and be pressured by them to meet all kinds of oddball men. And if she didn't go to meet them, she would have to bear her parents' philosophical blather.

"In this world, it seems it has to be one man and one woman together in order to be considered normal. I have enough trouble getting along with myself. I can't imagine having to get along with a man for a whole lifetime. What is love? Does love only mean eating, drinking, pooping, peeing and sleeping together? I'm anxious, too, but I'm anxious to find love, not anxious to marry someone. And I don't care if I *am* already thirty!" Xiaopin looked at Yuchuan picking up the bowls and chopsticks, and like a very bold man, Xiaopin let her gaze meander from Yuchuan's face to her chest, then down to her waist. "Yuchuan, I really envy you—so pretty, and with such a simple heart."

Yuchuan responded, smiling, "I can't tell if you're praising me or belittling me." The edge of her vision brushed past Lao Wu's face. She discovered he was also looking at her from head to foot, but so timidly it was almost painful.

Xiaopin continued, "Once a boyfriend of mine told me about his theory of love: 'love earlier and marry later; love more and marry less; just love and don't marry.' Back then I thought, how the hell did

I get mixed up with a creep like this? Now I think he's not such a jerk after all. If once in a lifetime a person can love just a few times with complete passion and abandon, or even just once, that's worth far more than getting married."

That night, Xiaopin talked with Yuchuan until the late hours, saying that all her troubles were because she couldn't be like Yuchuan, putting love, marriage and daily life all into a "three in one." Their conversation gradually shifted to Lao Wu.

"Lao Wu has never had dealings with women. Who knows if he has ever loved anyone in his heart secretly. I really hope that he has never experienced that sort of hidden love, because that kind of one-sided secret love must be a cause for despair. It could only hurt him. He wouldn't express it. He knows he doesn't have the capacity to follow through on a love affair to the end. So even if he did love someone, he could only hold it inside and not express it, not give it any possibility to develop. He has never said anything about this to me. And if this guy doesn't tell you something himself, don't even *think* of trying to investigate a single trace of it."

Xiaopin had now been asleep next to her for a long time. Yuchuan could still hear Lao Wu's hushed bustling. Yuchuan looked to the neighboring bed and concentrated her gaze on Xiaopin's profile. The orange-colored streetlight pushed its way in through the window, and in the midst of the dimness, Xiaopin's silhouette was so graceful that Yuchuan used it to outline a reclining Lao Wu. In the most exquisite and fine part of everyone in this family, there existed a Lao Wu.

When Cai Yao called once again to say he was going to delay the date of his return further, Yuchuan did not complain. Every night, she and Lao Wu would sit on the balcony to enjoy the cool air with practically nothing to talk about, but in that atmosphere her heart felt gradually moved. That feeling made her hope that no one would come to disturb them.

"Lao Wu, do you like swimming?"

"Not too much."

"I like it."

"Oh."

Lao Wu had a way of not letting you bring up any topic. He never gave you any "really?" or "why?" or "how could that be?"—any of those verbal openings that give you an opportunity to continue or to start a new topic. Sometimes she felt he was looking at her. Stealthily she would turn her face and find that it was true. She would then look back at him more directly as if to say: this time you really must say something. But he was still as quiet as before. Then she thought, what if he were to talk and started babbling about this and that, just like normal people. Would that inexpressible feeling still be there? Yuchuan no longer expected him to open his mouth. She felt him look at her, but she didn't return his gaze in the same manner, because she knew he could not digest her looking back. His shy appreciation of her could only persist if she refrained from approaching or disturbing him in the midst of his observation and enjoyment.

Toward evening of the day before Cai Yao was to return, Yuchuan went to a nearby public swimming pool to swim. The water was crammed full of people. Swimming even a little distance meant bumping into someone or being bumped into. Everyone was splashing about in the water, chatting and laughing, soaking in the coolness. On summer evenings this was the cheapest cool place. As Yuchuan was approaching the side of the pool and preparing to get out, suddenly she heard someone yell "Hooligan!" Yuchuan looked over and saw men and women in the pool jostling together in a flesh-colored knot, seizing and beating someone. The piercing voice of a young woman floated over with a "wung-wung" reverberation: "Creep! Following me every day! You followed me from the street to the tram, then you followed me here! You think a chicken-boned creep like you can take advantage of *me?!*" The crowd shouted in high spirits, feeling that if they didn't get in at least two licks apiece, they'd be missing out. Like people fighting with each other to buy cheap goods, they had to thrust their hands out fast, otherwise their "strike" would come up empty. Heaving a sigh, Yuchuan stepped out of the pool, but suddenly she discovered the one being held was Lao Wu, and her brain swelled for a moment.

"What are you *doing?!* Let him go!" Suddenly Yuchuan found herself poised between Lao Wu and the flying fists, though she had no recollection of how she had jumped back into the pool and pierced fishlike through the human netting.

Lao Wu stood expressionless, enduring the blood that was trickling from his nostrils into his mouth, enduring her protecting and embracing him. When the water droplets flowed from the tips of his hair into his eyes, he squeezed them shut for a moment.

"That hooligan! He's been following me for days now!" The girl yelling was eighteen or nineteen, her attractive face grown turbulent from fury.

"Him? He's been behaving like a hooligan toward you? Following you? Dream on—I spend every day together with him!" Yuchuan knew that her own face was turbulent as well and used it to best effect. "I'm his girlfriend! Everybody look at me—am I such a horrible creature? If he has me, why would he play the hooligan with you? Would it even be worth his trouble?"

People gazed at her for an instant, then started murmuring. Most of them were annoyed at having been taken in, at having put out effort for such a conceited young woman, at having wasted a few punches and kicks. Some people even started to sympathize with Lao Wu, randomly giving opinions about how to stop the bleeding.

When they got out of the pool, Yuchuan used her fingers to pinch the base and bridge of his nose, making him half recline in her arms. Quietly she told him, it's all right, turn and lie this way; after a while the bleeding will stop, just trust this nursing school graduate. Her eyes intercepted all the curious gazes and ran them off. It was the first time she had ever realized her eyes could be so fierce, shrewish, ferocious. As soon as the bleeding stopped, Lao Wu became restless on Yuchuan's lap. She still coaxed him in his ear, don't move, stay there like a good boy, lean back and rest a while. He closed his eyes, and Yuchuan saw under his thin eyelids that his eyeballs rolled and darted hesitatingly. She didn't ask him a single thing. Did you really do anything to that girl, did you really follow her around here and there like a scoundrel? Are you really as rascally and low-down as she said? She raised none of this. She only asked, are you cold? The sun has gone down. When the wind blows, you probably feel cold, don't you? Come, I'll warm you up. He did not reply. His whole bodily form shrank, even shriveled. In his shrinking he seemed to want to make the sharp outlines of his bones more indistinct, or at least less obvious. Maybe he was recoiling from his own foolish intentions toward the girl, from his hopeless furtive pursuit of her. She wanted to tell him, take heart, be bold, call out to her as if giving orders: I love you! Listen to me, dammit, I love you! Then rush at her like a bandit, just as Cai Yao has said and done to me. She also wanted to say, how can you be so numb to your own originality, to your own wonderful traits that others find so attractive?

She said nothing. Touching his skin, as delicate as a girl's, she bent double and strained to pull his body up to hers, up to where her chest came under his chin. He opened his eyes as if to figure out where he was and where his body had gotten itself to.

Yuchuan avoided his eyes. In the face of his fragility, her vitality, fullness and life expectancy, so much longer than his, made her feel guilty.

"You're cold, aren't you? When you lose blood, you get cold easily. If I warm you up like this, do you feel better?"

He responded with an affirmative "uhn." Yuchuan could hear his self-loathing and embarrassment. She used her towel to wipe the remaining water droplets off his body. Her heart held so much regret: he really should have been such a handsome and proud young man. He should have been too proud to even take a second look at her. And she should have had the freedom to pursue him, to love him, even if the love could have no result, even if it was doomed to be a love as short-lived as he—if only she weren't his brother's fiancée. He should have been able to enjoy a woman's body, even for just a moment as fleeting as the morning dew. She would have loved to give him this enjoyment if there hadn't been a Cai Yao between them.

When Cai Yao, returning from the provinces, came barging

through the front door, he hugged her right in front of Lao Wu, and only after he had embraced her for a full two minutes did he greet anyone else.

Lao Wu walked away. Yuchuan felt he walked off a little regretfully and a little guiltily.

Cai Yao hummed a completely mangled version of a popular song as he stepped into the shower. The shower made a sloshing sound. After a while he shouted, "Hey, Yuchuan, hand me a towel!" Soon he called out again: "Excuse me, could you bring me my undershorts?" She scrupulously avoided looking at his well-proportioned, robust unyielding nakedness. She could not stand to compare his body with Lao Wu's.

In a flash Cai Yao had bolted the bathroom door, and its "clack" sound reverberated throughout the apartment.

"No! I don't want to! Lao Wu's at home!" she protested in a low voice, but she was pressed against the door.

"Never mind Lao Wu."

She wanted to say, isn't Lao Wu a human being? Or is he a piece of livestock or furniture, so if you want to do something you don't have to take him into account? You don't have to consider his feelings, that he might get upset, huh? Cai Yao suddenly seemed like a stranger. How could someone be so healthy, almost as if he were shamelessly usurping a portion of vitality not his own — Lao Wu's portion.

The door started to shudder. Yuchuan could not get him off her and feared that too fierce a struggle would make an even louder din. She just asked him to go lightly, lightly. Then she heard the front door go "ponk." That was Lao Wu's statement that he didn't want to prevent their happy noises. At that moment, her whole being was diffused with uneasiness and revulsion.

At the end of the year, Cai Yao still had not been assigned an apartment. Father and Mother started making plans to have someone come in to build a new door to Cai Yao's room. Father joked with

Yuchuan at the dinner table: "Look how close it is. Da Mao only has to take three steps to take you over the threshold of the bridal chamber." Mother said having a May wedding and giving birth to a child in March of the following year meant that both happy events would catch the good season, one at either end. Without knowing why, at that moment Yuchuan looked toward Lao Wu. She found that Lao Wu was also looking at her.

Before Spring Festival, while reading the evening paper, Yuchuan discovered a very small announcement: "One-Man Exhibition of Paintings by Cai Wu to be held on X Day of X Month at X Gallery." Yuchuan jumped up and knocked on Lao Wu's door: "Lao Wu, Lao Wu!" When he opened, she pointed to the newspaper and asked him, "Is this you?"

"Uhn."

"You're so great—a solo exhibition!"

Lao Wu seemed not to know why she was talking so loudly and excitedly.

"Why, you! Why is it you've never breathed a word of this? No one in this household even knows!"

"Don't *you* know?" He pursed his lips slightly and pushed out a smile. That was the first time Yuchuan had seen that Lao Wu could show his teeth when he smiled, both sardonically and a little rascally. At that moment he resembled Cai Yao.

The day the exhibition started, Yuchuan couldn't get off work until the afternoon. It was quite difficult to get directions to the gallery's location. It was in the basement of a music hall. The old man taking tickets at the door had dozed off. After he was awakened by the sound of Yuchuan's high heels, he said, "Oh, you're the tenth person today."

"Aren't there many people coming?"

"Well, it's better than nobody. I understand a little bit about painting. I've met painters and craftsmen of practically every style and school. But paintings like the ones this fellow paints, I just don't understand." The old man laughed self-importantly and wagged his head in cadence. "Master Baishi once said, 'If a painting is too representational, it simply pleases convention; too little so, and it just fools the world.'" Without waiting for the sales transaction to be completed, Yuchuan had already walked into the exhibition hall.

The gallery was long and narrow, and inside the picture frames hanging on either side there seemed to be people, animals and plants. But Yuchuan couldn't tell whether she had guessed correctly or not. She looked at them all in turn and finally she saw him, sitting all alone at the far end—Lao Wu. He stood up. He knew she had not come to see the paintings.

"It's pretty quiet at the moment," she said.

"It's been quiet the whole time."

"You're probably not like other painters, sending invitations to the four corners of the earth, right?"

"I sent out a few."

"They'll come tomorrow. Tomorrow is Sunday!"

Lao Wu smiled, as if smiling at a child playing make-believe to fool herself and others. Yuchuan walked along the long and narrow gallery and looked again at each of the paintings. She forced herself to stand a decent interval of time in front of each one. All along the way, she commented on the uniqueness of each, without resorting to clichés. But she knew Lao Wu did not take her comments seriously and had no interest in her perfunctory critique. That type of critique could have been used for anything: a tasty dish, a hair style, a fashionable outfit. When they said goodbye, she was at one end of the gallery and he at the other.

That evening, Yuchuan braved the snow flurries and ran to many of her hospital co-workers' homes to implore them to go see the exhibition. One co-worker knew some Americans who were in town to install medical equipment and train personnel, and Yuchuan practically forced her to make a telephone call to invite them. On Sunday morning when Lao Wu, sitting quietly, saw a group of people of all types and colors pour into the gallery, he was so startled that one buttock slipped off his chair. Yuchuan, waiting outside the door for two newspaper reporters she had arranged to meet, saw how Lao Wu's hand was caught up by each visitor's hand, grasped, then shaken a few times. Even though he returned the courtesy, his facial expression was scattered and confused. Yuchuan could see he was hiding a deep annoyance: how could such a tranquil place suddenly turn into a temple festival?

The two reporters arrived carrying all types of photographic equipment. Yuchuan put on her most charming smile to receive them, with a "you've gone to so much trouble" here and a "thank you so much" there. The two reporters, who had been hanging around in high society so long they had become blasé, replied with a chuckle, "No need to thank us. Afterward, we're all going to get treated to a fancy meal! Aren't they all like that these days? Everybody's three parts showmanship and seven parts flattery! If it's an occasion for everybody to have a good time and then go out for a nice meal, then it's certainly a good deal!"

Yuchuan cooled her tone of voice: "He's different."

The two reporters reacted to Yuchuan's suddenly hurt feelings with incomprehension and even a bit of disappointment. "Well, then, what do you want us to do?" one of them asked, his voice having dropped an octave.

"You don't have to do anything. Uh . . . just walk in and tell him you're reporters, and that his paintings have attracted a lot of acclaim." Yuchuan was thinking as she spoke. "And tell him he paints very well, that his exhibition is a great success, that he has great potential. Just tell him these things. Afterward, I'll take you out to eat. You choose any restaurant you like."

She could tell that the reporters wanted to get to the bottom of this charade, but Yuchuan did not reveal her motives. "Let's just say I'm pleading with you, all right? Later, when you go to the hospital to see the dentist, I'll get you an appointment."

The reporters stole a sly look at each other, not daring to stir up more trouble with Yuchuan, who was already so hurt she looked nearly tragic. They walked in like actors getting into character and going on stage. Yuchuan saw them both affect looking at each painting and knitting their brows, murmuring, their facial expressions earnest. Finally, one after the other they walked over to Lao Wu. First they showed their press credentials, then, very professionally, they shook his hand and exchanged polite greetings with him. She saw Lao Wu's face turn pale upon hearing the two of them recite their lines just as she had instructed them. When they came out, they saw Yuchuan waiting for them outside. They screwed up their faces. "Where did they dig up a character like that? He even put price tags on the paintings, but they're not selling. As if anybody would pay good money for those outlandish things! He's probably the only one who calls them paintings!"

Only after everyone began to disperse did Lao Wu see Yuchuan behind the curtain of people. Since it was closing time, he was preparing to leave the gallery. She didn't ask anything: Were there many people today? Did any reporters or foreign guests arrive? She feared he would peer through the ripped seams, see through this vain spectacle, see clearly that it was she who had counterfeited this triumphant day.

"Shall we go out for a walk?" Yuchuan suggested.

In his hesitation and surprise, Lao Wu nodded.

Lao Wu led the way, as Yuchuan was not familiar with the city. Lao Wu led her in silence. People became more and more sparse, and the snow underfoot became cleaner and cleaner. In front of them was the moat of the old city, and beside it were some saplings.

"I planted these trees!"

Yuchuan followed him into the small, sparse grove. She turned back to look at the city's hubbub and lights and felt a very sweet loneliness. The slope under her shoes was not too easy to negotiate, so Lao Wu gave her his hand to support her. They stood hand in hand on the moat's stone embankment.

"Would you dare to jump?" Yuchuan asked in jest. But in fact she was not speaking purely in jest.

"Jump into the moat? What for?"

"Let's say that on the other side of the moat there were a desert island: no people, or only people who don't know us, and over there everything could begin anew. Would you jump?"

Lao Wu didn't speak. Yuchuan felt his hand, which was holding her hand, gradually become stiff, mechanical.

"Lao Wu, if I weren't . . . me, that is, if I were just myself, just a girl named Yuchuan, things would be different, right? Yuchuan would love you. If there were a place to run, a place where you were just you and I were just me, so nothing between us could be called a scandal, would you be willing to run away to that place?" Lao Wu's hand released her hand.

That evening while Yuchuan was in the kitchen washing dishes by herself, Cai Yao came up behind her and stretched out his hands to hug her. She saw square-fingernailed, square-knuckled, strong-muscled hands reaching for her breasts and shrieked, "Let me go!"

Yuchuan was transferred to in-patient care and started working night shifts. When she got off work, the whole family was asleep, and only in Lao Wu's room was there still slight noise and movement. One night she tapped on the door a couple of times, and the door opened much faster than she had expected.

"I just wanted to see what you were up to." Yuchuan leaned on the door frame. Almost soundlessly she asked, "May I come in?"

"I'm writing something . . . "

"You're not painting?"

"I don't paint much any more. I've already held the exhibition."

"I'd like to see your studio."

Suddenly, as if making a decision, Lao Wu asked, "Do you have time?"

Yuchuan cast her eyes upward a moment, apparently concentrated on figuring out a time, but in reality she was hesitating, casting about for an escape route. She knew that something was going to happen. From Lao Wu's eyes she saw that he understood this as well.

"Is it far?"

"Not far, just hard to find. If you give me a time, I can wait for you at the bus stop." Lao Wu spoke quickly, his speed sealing off both their escape routes.

At two in the afternoon, Yuchuan arrived at the bus stop. There was no sign of Lao Wu. Yuchuan stood there enduring the poplar blossoms falling on her face and body. A poplar blossom pricked her eye, and no matter how much she rubbed it, it still irritated her. She pulled out a compact mirror and carefully plucked out its residue. In the mirror she saw that her lipstick had smeared into a red streak from the corner of her mouth across her cheek. Because of it, her whole face looked in disarray. Perhaps just now when she rubbed her eyes, her movements had been flustered, and her hand had rubbed her lips. Or maybe on the bus when people were pushing and crowding, some back or arm or elbow, attempting to clear a larger space for itself, had caused that red spot. A powdered face, once stained with something, is not easily wiped clean. She used saliva on her handkerchief to wipe the stain off, but after she'd rubbed the red streak clean, her facial color was uneven. Still, she didn't have the courage to apply lipstick and powder right there on the street. After all, she wasn't accustomed to putting on makeup. So why had she applied such heavy lipstick and such thick powder in the first place? Was it to blot out forever a pure and innocent Yuchuan? Or was the purpose of such thick powder to seal in forever a pure Yuchuan in a state without fault or blame? She saw the depths of the mirror reflecting this mottled face, this besmirching desire. Last night, when they had agreed on the time and place they were to meet, the excitement and fear of each was a warning to the other. Something was going to happen, and what was to happen would change the nature of their lives from this time forward.

Yuchuan snapped the mirror shut and put it away. In it she encapsulated the image of herself before her fall, shut it up inside, preserved it. The sky was filled with poplar blossoms, lively as living things, flying helter-skelter, playing and chasing people. They looked like snow, yet snow had no equivalent for their commotion and mischief.

Lao Wu had not come. Having waited half an hour, Yuchuan wiped off her lipstick and powder and crossed the street to wait for the bus going back. Her heart had both lost and gained something. It felt empty and clean. She would be able to concentrate with complete composure throughout the night shift. When the bus was about to leave the stop, she saw a long delicate shadow appear at the place where she had just been standing. This shadow looked not at all as if it had just arrived, but rather had been waiting for quite some time. Waiting as though it had taken root.

One day after Yuchuan had gotten off work, she saw Cai Yao waiting for her in front of the apartment building.

"I have to tell you, don't worry too much about this, but we've lost two hundred *yuan* at home. My mother never pays much attention to the small royalty payments my father gets. She just puts them in a drawer and spends the money without ever counting it. But these two hundred *yuan* were Xiaopin's. She gave them to Ma for safekeeping. She wanted to buy a new bicycle. My mother doesn't count the money used for daily expenses, but this money is Xiaopin's, and she recalls very clearly that she never touched it."

"Something like this is enough to make a daughter-in-law-to-be like me just want to die of shame!" Yuchuan's temper tossed out. "I told you from the beginning that we shouldn't live at your parents' house. I told you to move. Even if it were only a melon trellis, I would still live there with you. But, no, like people with no face, we had to go sponge off others. And now I *really* feel like I have no face!"

"I *told* you not to worry about this too much! Ma only told this to me, and of course she doesn't suspect you or me."

"So who *does* she suspect?"

"Ma doesn't want to suspect anybody."

"Maybe your dad spent it. He forgot to count it, then he forgot about it afterward." Yuchuan hadn't lived in this household for long before she had determined that this was not one of those normal families where the wife asks the husband about all his outside activities. There were women constantly telephoning, and Father would answer with a couple of short clipped phrases and then walk out the door. Mother had never raised a fuss over this. "Maybe your dad needed money for something he couldn't talk about."

"Don't go making wild guesses. You're still not clear on some of our family matters . . . When we get into the house, don't say anything. Just pretend you don't know."

At dinner, Lao Wu was the first to get up from his seat and put down his fifty *fen* as usual. Yuchuan noticed that it was Xiaopin who first stopped chewing, then Cai Yao stopped moving his chopsticks, then Mother put down her bowl. All three of them watched him put on his jacket and hat, and all three were fearful and apprehensive. Father had no reaction, but his chopsticks kept shuttling mechanically between the same plate and his mouth. Once Lao Wu had gone out the door, Xiaopin said, as if to herself, that exhibition he put on must have cost a lot of money. Cai Yao interrupted, his speech also sounding like a soliloquy: taking money from your own household is not too big a deal, but if you were to do such a thing on the outside, it would be a serious matter. Mother, stupefied with remorse, reproached herself: it's all my fault that I didn't lock it up. After that, oppressiveness and chagrin prevailed, as if this day had suddenly spoiled everyone's happiness; as if no one knew how to deal with this family's shameful secret, on their own or as a whole family. That night, each one of them dejectedly retired early. Yuchuan made excuses, saying there were some letters she had to write, and stayed alone in the living room.

When the door made a sound, she turned her head. Lao Wu walked over and showed her a few new chops he had just carved, saying that Cai Yao had implored him many times to carve some decorative chops to stamp on his book collection. She stared fixedly at his long, slender and soft fingers, noting their jarring whiteness. Only doing many devious things could give someone such jarringly white hands.

"Is there something wrong with me?" Lao Wu asked, meaning, why are you examining me so carefully?

"Do you need money?" Yuchuan looked deeply into his eyes.

Lao Wu did not seem to understand her question. His pursed lips opened slightly.

"I have some money I could give you," Yuchuan told his two

white hands. Those hands gradually withdrew from her field of vision. She felt his whole being was withdrawing.

"Lao Wu, except for you, everyone here knows: there's some money missing from the household." Yuchuan, short of breath, spoke in a flat tone.

"I know," he said. He wanted to say something else, but instead his Adam's apple just bobbed a few times.

Yuchuan wanted to ask: *what* do you know? You know you have taken the money yourself, or you know that you have been wrongly accused? Did you do this thing or didn't you? But he walked away hurriedly. His waist was still tilted, yet he walked very quickly. The next day Yuchuan worked the night shift and was idle at home during the day. As before the whole family in turn knocked at that door, calling, "Lao Wu!" Yuchuan could hear that this customary calling out had undergone a bit of a shift. Exasperation and disdain were now its major notes.

When Mother went to try the door, he had still not shown his face. Mother thought something was amiss and leaned on the door, calling out repeatedly. She called until Father slowly stood up from his dining-room chair. Unexpectedly, Mother discovered that the door wasn't locked from the inside. So she pushed it open. The room was empty and other than Lao Wu's smell, nothing else remained. Father suddenly fell backward into his chair.

Lao Wu had gone. He had not left behind so much as a word. Several days later the money was found. The envelope with the money was discovered stuck between two drawers, apparently as a result of the drawer being filled too full. Xiaopin looked at the two hundred-*yuan* bills and said they looked like the two original bills. Yuchuan felt everyone was pondering that "looked like."

Lao Wu never returned, although if he had, he would no longer have had to live in that little storeroom. Xiaopin moved into a university dormitory, and Cai Yao was assigned an apartment. To assuage their consciences, Father and Mother remodeled the room Xiaopin and Yuchuan had stayed in and called it hopefully "Lao Wu's Room." But the only news of Lao Wu was a little corner of a bookstore displaying several copies of a book on petroglyphs. Yuchuan went regularly to see whether anyone was buying them. They grew old in mint condition.

Father had a brainstorm and called the small publishing house that had published Lao Wu's book, asking for the author's address. "He has no address." The person answering was the managing editor.

Annoyed, Father pounded on the table, trying to convey his power and prestige over the telephone line. "You *must* be able to find a way to locate his address!" Yuchuan was rather moved, thinking fathers will be fathers. She had been adamant about delaying the wedding date, because of a mysterious expectation in her heart. This time Father, still holding the telephone, said, "Tell me. I'm listening." Gradually, his ear started to recoil from the receiver and two tears ran down from the corners of his eyes.

Two weeks before, Lao Wu had died of illness in a district hospital. All his royalties had been used to pay his medical bills. He had left nothing for this family, nor had he taken anything from it.

Not long after the wedding, Cai Yao in his cups tearfully told Yuchuan he had had affairs with two other women. After crying, he smiled again and lightly stroked Yuchuan's face around her expressionless lusterless eyes and asked, "Do you know which of those decorative chops Lao Wu carved for me I like the most?" Not receiving her attention, he answered himself: "The one with the inscription *Nothing More than Male and Female*." He said he had stamped that one on all his novels. The words exposed the root of all trouble: nothing more than male and female. He stared blankly, and the smile on his face was a bit silly. "Lao Wu is lucky. He never walked into that place, then he just turned around and walked straight out." Slowly, in an emotional state that bore less and less logic, he fell asleep.

Once a month he would get roaring drunk like this and would tell a bit of truth. Yuchuan lightly removed his arm from its resting place on her neck. Her eyes quivered, and two teardrops flowed down like a sudden rain. The haziness of the lamp looked like the fog of memory. Fast asleep, Cai Yao had a pursed mouth and sharp precipitous cheeks. Drunkenness gave his whole person a Lao Wu-like gentleness.

At least in this way Lao Wu could live again, live again before her eyes and at her breast: live in the gentleness of his brother's drunken state.

Notes to "Nothing More Than Male and Female"

Page 123 **Yuchuan:** pronounced "yh chwan," this name has the characters for "rain" and "river." The second character, which is the same as the second character in the name of the province Sichuan (literally "four rivers") indicates that she probably comes from there.

Page 123 **Cai Yao:** Cai (pronounced "tsai") is the family surname. *Yao* means "bright" or "shining."

Page 123 **Lao Wu:** literally "Old Five." Household nickname typically given to the fifth son or fifth child.

Page 123 **Spring festival:** the preferred name in mainland China for Chinese New Year, which occurs in late January or early February.

Page 124 **Xiaopin:** pronounced "shyao pin," this is an erudite name referring to a short piece of music or drama.

Page 126 **Da Mao:** "big hairy." It is common for Chinese families to call children by nicknames, some of them almost derogatory. Since infant mortality was historically very high, the superstition developed that calling a child by a different (preferably unflattering) name would cause the King of Death to pass over the child and not carry it off.

Page 127 **"or did you meet a tiger on the way?":** untranslatable rhyme in the original—Lao Wu rhymes with *laohu*, the word for tiger.

Page 134 **Stone chops:** stone seals that are dipped in thick red ink to stamp official documents or to show ownership.

Page 144 **"he hugged her right in front of Lao Wu":** in Chinese culture, openly displaying affection in the presence of others is simply "not done."

Page 145 **Cai Wu:** Lao Wu's proper name. The character "Wu" in this name means "enlightened" or "awakened."

Page 151 **Yuan:** the Chinese unit of currency, sometimes also called the *renminbi* (RMB). At the time in which this story is set, a typical factory worker in a Chinese city had a take-home pay of about 100 *yuan* a month.

少女小漁 Siao Yu

They say that the women who exit the train stations in the suburbs of Sydney between three and four in the afternoon are all stocky, fierce, low-heeled, dressed in segmented utilitarian clothing and carry an excessively complex body odor that stuffs one's sinuses.

They also say that the women who exit the train stations between four and five are fundamentally different women. They are all dressed in hose and high heels, and even as their makeup is starting to spoil, their expressions remain dignified. Their gait is poised, buttocks large and small rolling perfectly round inside tight skirts.

The first wave of women has been released from various factories; the second has descended from the office towers. Chinese people in Sydney call them "female workers" and "office ladies." And yet, the former live no worse than the latter. Living well or not living well in Sydney, this city of the simple and silly life, all depends on how much you earn. The female workers earn more than the office ladies, and they don't have to follow the latest fashions in dresses, shoes and stockings. They use their money to eat, to live, to save up for major purchases. For instance, female workers never wear imitation jewelry; it's all real gold, real diamonds, real jade. Even before you get close, the glow from their bodies screams at you.

Moreover, after the female workers have gone home and taken a shower, shedding their clothing as if molting a skin, the office ladies are still encased in their clothes and makeup. By the time the office ladies walk out of the turnstile at the train station, the female workers have become fully human again. They've changed into loose comfortable house dresses, their bodies less restrained in this kind of clothing than if they wore nothing at all, and have gone to the market to look for bargains. At that hour, the markets sell certain vegetables, fruit and meat that cannot keep much longer. They sell at a price approaching "pure communism." In this way, the female workers have yet another advantage over the office ladies: they pick up all their groceries cheaply, leaving none of the bargains for "them."

And yet the female workers hope one day to be office ladies, to wear high heels, to put on tight skirts, to deface their own features with makeup. And if that means imitation jewelry, so be it; and if that means no more inexpensive groceries, then so be it.

Siao Yu was standing at the train station, two plastic bags at her sides filled with a few vegetables and some meat for which she had just spent her last few dollars. Next to her were other women like herself who had just bought groceries and, on the way home, had gone to meet their husbands at the train station. Only Siao Yu's husband was not really her husband. (How to explain something like this?) The sixty-seven-year-old man with whom she had gone to the marriage registry office had no connection with her at all. What could she have in common with an old man? And with *him*? A degenerate old Italian with the skin of his belly folded in layers like a terraced field? Siao Yu was only twenty-two — would she want a husband whose age exceeded hers by half a century? This was, of course, a ruse well known to the immigration authorities. Siao Yu paid money, and the old man sold his citizenship. The two of them conspired together against the law, but after all, it wasn't their government. Everybody did this, and the Immigration Department couldn't possibly have enough manpower to pursue every couple. Besides, it was said that in this country, no matter if young women married old men or young women married old *women,* the government would still wish them well.

Another group of passengers came out of the station, and Siao Yu craned her neck to look. She was neither tall nor large, yet she had the chest and buttocks of a tall or large woman; there was a certain voluptuousness about her. Everybody thinks that this kind of woman is ideal for giving birth and raising children, suffering hardship and working hard, but she doesn't have much of a brain. A little less brain but a little more heart. Otherwise how could Siao Yu have become a nurse when she was only seventeen? On the Mainland (she had long since grown accustomed to referring to the Chinese Motherland as "the Mainland") she had nursed those patients that no one paid attention to, and before they died, they all said she had a good heart. When she got the chance to go abroad, people said, what a fitting reward! People would kill to go abroad, but Siao Yu migrated to Sydney just like walking outside for a breath of fresh air.

When Siao Yu saw him coming out of the station, she smiled. People said that Siao Yu smiled especially well because she smiled with no ulterior motive.

His name was Jiang Wei. Ten years ago in China he had won the nation's first prize for breast stroke, known in Chinese as the "frog stroke," and even now he sported beautiful froglike muscles and skin. When he had met Siao Yu, he was just about to leave China, and this friend and that friend had already started to organize goodbye parties for him. They had joked with him, after you've hung out there and become half-foreign, don't forget to haul your buddies out too! Siao Yu had been brought along by someone and didn't know anyone well. But if anyone invited her to dance, she would dance. If they held her close, she was close, and if they kept her at a distance, she was at a distance: she smiled all the same. When Jiang Wei's hands started to wander from her waist, she smiled in acknowledgment. When Jiang Wei went a step further, she raised her face and asked,

"What are you doing?" It was as though she were the only one who didn't know that men are at times idle and indecent. He asked her name, where she worked and such, then invited her to go out with him on the weekend.

"Okay," she replied, neither enthusiastically nor apathetically.

On Sunday he brought her over to his house and had her sit for an hour, but no one in the house had any plans to free up a little space for them. The only thing he could do was take her out. One after another, they went to two or three parks, but nowhere could they escape other people's eyes. Siao Yu uttered not a word of complaint. He wondered aloud where all the crowds came from, and she walked a long way with him as they changed locations. Finally, when it was already dark, they returned to his place. Drawing her behind the gate to the common courtyard, he embraced her this way and that way for a while. He asked her, "Do you like to be with me this way?" She didn't answer; whatever shape her body was kneaded into was fine with her. The second week, they went to bed together. After the busy part was over, Jiang Wei dozed off. Half awake, he asked her, "The first time you went to bed with someone, who was it?"

Siao Yu said slowly, "With a patient, right before he died. He had liked me for more than a year."

"He liked you, so you just *let* him?" Jiang Wei said, tensing from the roots of his hair down to his toes. Siao Yu could read from his eyes: do you owe men that much? Are you worth so little? Her hands, carrying her heart's thoughts, stroked his body's taut, froglike flesh. "It was as if he thirsted for me. He seemed to be suffering so much, the poor man." She used her eyes to say the remaining sentence: weren't you just like that, too, a moment ago? As if I had food that could satisfy your hunger?

Jiang Wei had been gone for half a year and hadn't written her a word. Then one day he sent a package with all different kinds of paper, saying he had already arranged her school registration and bought her a plane ticket, and all she would have to do was to carry this packet of papers to the Australian consulate. That's how she came to get on a plane to a place so far away, "eight thousand *li* of clouds and moonlight." She was neither particularly elated nor despondent. When she was about to board the plane, her large over-filled suitcase suddenly popped open. Her mother, seeing she was the only one left in the departure lounge, got angry: "You're going to miss your flight! How can you be so lackadaisical?" Siao Yu raised her head and smiled first, then replied with that mellow voice of hers, "Don't you see that I'm hurrying?"

When they started living together, Jiang Wei would work in the morning and go to class in the afternoon, while Siao Yu would work all day during the week and go to classes on weekends. The two of them had only dinnertime to spend together. That time was crammed: they had to eat, converse, be intimate. Though there was every variety of food and intimacy, as far as conversation went, there was only one topic: when we get permanent residence, we'll do this and that. So, quite naturally, their talk would wind around to immigration status. Jiang Wei would often smile sneakily and say, "Why don't you go marry some foreigner?"

"Over here aren't *you* a foreigner?" she said. She immediately discovered this was the wrong thing to say to him.

"What? You're calling me a foreigner? Do you mean that, just because I don't have permanent residence, I'm some kind of foreigner? Do you?" In his frustration he pushed her away from himself. Given their small apartment, he could only keep her at a psychological distance.

Siao Yu was silent. She let him decide when to cross over the abyss. Soon he came, asking rhetorically, "Do you think I could bear to marry you off to some foreigner?" Siao Yu suddenly discovered a secret: in his eyes, she was a beautiful woman, beautiful beyond compare. When she looked at herself, she felt she was rather plain. She had never stared for long into the mirror because she felt so plain. She spent neither time nor money on her appearance. She was quite unlike other women, fiercely intent on adorning themselves like Christmas trees. On the weekend, all the dimsum restaurants and shops in Chinatown were bedazzled with these "trees," and everywhere you looked seemed like a Christmas-tree forest.

A friend of Jiang Wei's actually found an underground organization that specialized in matchmaking between the unlikeliest of cou-
ples. "It costs $15,000," the friend warned. But Jiang Wei acted out of
desperation. What else could have driven him to scrounge up enough
money from God knows where to have a girl like Siao Yu go through
such humiliation? Just the idea of standing, even for a short time,
side by side with such a pig before the magistrate would drive most
girls crazy. Not to mention having to go to various offices with him to
be stared at and interrogated. The girls are supposed to report glibly
on distinguishing characteristics of the man's private parts. And then
there is the marriage vow, embracing, and kissing not just once but
twice or three times. So why not find a man who's not such a pig? But
only piglike men were left over to enter sham marriages. Besides, the
more piglike the man, the lower the price. Fifteen thousand dollars,
and the old man was neither lame nor blind; that's a good deal.
That's how Jiang Wei presented it to Siao Yu.

Standing in front of the semicircular counter at the marriage registry office, shoulder to shoulder and holding hands with the old
man, Siao Yu didn't feel all that frightened. In any case, she didn't
understand the lines she had previously rehearsed for the occasion.
Things that you don't understand leave no impression on you; they
just trip off the lips and tongue with your consciousness far, far away,
completely unmoved.

Meanwhile Jiang Wei's bridal party of fake friends and relatives
stood off to one side. Before the ceremony, each time someone sang
"Zhong Kui marries off his Little Sister," or "Fan Li relinquishes Xi
Shi," he laughed, but eventually anyone who teased him would get a
glare back in return.

During the ceremony, Siao Yu did not turn her head back to look
at Jiang Wei. If she had, she would have known that he badly needed
her to look at him at that moment. He stood among the group of yellow-skinned "friends and relatives," his Adam's apple bobbing up
and down furiously, the froglike muscles on his body bulging out all
over, straining the seams on his thrift-store suit. She only looked at
the old man when absolutely necessary. He had had his hair dyed

before the ceremony and had invoiced this item to Siao Yu as well. Adding to this the rental of a suit and the purchase of a bottle of men's cologne, the old man had rooked her out of a total of a hundred dollars. She found out later that Rita had dyed the old man's hair and that Rita had also altered a suit for him that he used to wear decades ago while performing music.

Rita and the old man had a coarse yet rather moving relationship. Rita accompanied the old man in drinking wine, shedding tears, thinking of the old country and in sleeping. He played the violin and she sang, even though she sang off-key. The old man's most valuable possession was that violin. It didn't have a shoulder support, and he had not yet gone to find a replacement, because if he couldn't find an equally fine wood, then it would affect the violin's tone, at least that's the way the old man explained it: who knows? So the violin without a shoulder support rested against his shoulder, which wasn't very effective, so the neck of the violin kept slipping downward, even down below his waist. As a result, he assumed a melancholy posture as he played.

The old man was desperately poor yet had never gone to play on the streets for money. No matter how much Rita urged him, he wouldn't go. Instead, he had sold himself to Siao Yu. According to his own calculations, if he didn't drink himself to death first, he had at least another good ten years. And if he sold himself every two years, he would make ten thousand dollars each time, so that during the time remaining to him, he wouldn't have to live on thin air. From this perspective, even deducting the five-thousand-dollar commission for the underworld "matchmaking," it was a fairly clean and fairly lucrative way to earn a living.

After blowing the hundred dollars, the old rascal didn't look quite so rascally. Siao Yu noticed that his hair was like lacquer and was combed in a very old-fashioned pompadour. The cologne masked the odor of alcohol on his body. He wore his suit rather nattily, even a bit jauntily. The expression in his eyes was terribly earnest—his eyebrows had also been dyed and combed, like two shade hedges planted on his face. You could almost describe him as righteous and solemn. From the constant contractions of his lips, Siao Yu could see that his breathing was short from nervousness. At the end, the old man embraced her and kissed her according to custom. Seeing his old face press down toward hers, she became sad. At such an advanced age, she thought, still performing in such a parody. But the role was too heavy for him. He was already so tired he was gasping for air. Such a pity, she thought, after living to such an age, he can only play a groom in this farce, and he'll never have a chance to be a real groom again—never again be able to have this hope. And in fact he played the role so authentically, with such a craving, that he took his performance toward hyperrealism.

When the old man's dry cold lips touched hers, she couldn't bear to look at him any more. What was it that kept him from being a happy father and grandfather? There wasn't a single person standing behind him; all the wedding revelers were yellow-skinned, all on her side. He was really that extremely alone. Even Rita didn't come, because if she had, who would she be? When Siao Yu opened her eyes again, she saw in the old man's face a trace of pity as he asked himself, who would ruin such a pure and innocent girl as this?

After they had walked through the whole scenario, the guests rushed the "May-December couple" down to the lawn outside to take some pictures. Siao Yu and the old man got their picture taken in front of a Mercedes-Benz that the group happened to find parked near the edge of the lawn. Then, everyone else mobbed the car, saying "Take one of me, too." No matter what, in this life there is always a desire to possess, to brag, to show off, and one cannot do it without something to show. It was only Jiang Wei who wouldn't have his picture taken, as he slowly dragged along at the tail end of the crowd.

Only then did Siao Yu realize how unhappy Jiang Wei was. When the wedding party said goodbye to the old man, they used Chinese to make fun of him, saying such things as "Bye, bye, you old fart! You'd better stay in good shape, or we'll all pile into that little hut of yours . . ." Jiang Wei finally smiled, but it was a cruel smile.

That night when they got home, Siao Yu made dinner as usual. But Jiang Wei's chopsticks merely picked at his food. Finally he stopped the random conversation and told her to wipe off her lipstick. What lipstick? she asked. She had washed her face right after getting home. He put his chopsticks aside and yelled, "Go wipe it off!"

Siao Yu stared at him; she didn't know this person any more. Jiang Wei stormed into the bathroom, tore off a length of toilet paper, pinned her face with one hand and used force to wipe her lips, swabbing her nose and cheeks at the same time. Siao Yu thought, surely he must have seen that there were paper napkins on the table. She didn't struggle; she was scared to death that if she struggled, the anger from his repressed humiliation would vent itself without check. She wanted to cry, but seeing him with his head buried in her shoulder, sobbing with abandon, she felt his hurt was even deeper and more terrible than hers. Give him the chance to cry, she thought. Otherwise, if both cry, who will be left to give comfort? She used strength to shoulder his sobbing, his trembling, his grievance against heaven.

Early the next morning when Jiang Wei woke up to go to work, he kissed her. Afterward he looked up at the ceiling with a dazed expression and said, "Another 364 days left to go." Siao Yu knew what he was referring to. After one year, she could bring divorce proceedings and after a certain amount of time and a court appearance, she could regain her single status and withdraw from the dirty business of this marriage. But no matter how warm and affectionate Siao Yu was, from that time on she and Jiang Wei were a bit estranged—sharing a sort of odd resentment. At the moments of greatest happiness he might spout, "Are you being real with me? Or do you pretend it's real with everyone?" When he asked this, he was not threatening or fierce but weak and helpless, and it made Siao Yu's heart ache to no end. He was one of those men with a temper like a tiger's: if he wasn't fierce, it meant he wasn't normal. Now even his smile changed: the space between his eyebrows would draw together and the two lines beside his nose diverged oddly downward, looking at the same time awkward and depraved.

As soon as Jiang Wei saw Siao Yu standing at the station gate among those wives, he flashed one of his awkward smiles. They walked home together. As usual, Siao Yu did not point out to him that she was carrying two large shopping bags. And as usual, Jiang Wei did not notice this until they arrived at the ground floor of their building. "Hey, why didn't you ask me to carry them?" he said and snatched both bags away. Siao Yu smiled through her fatigue and climbed the stairs slowly after him.

Since part of the money they paid the old man and the organization was borrowed, they had moved three guys into their apartment to share the rent. The whole place smelled of feet. Just as Siao Yu was getting ready to clean the house and straighten things up, Jiang Wei said: "Did they pay you money to clean up after them?" One of the three guys worked cutting thread at a clothing factory, and little threads would stick all over his woolen shirt and drop all over the apartment. When Siao Yu started to pick them up, Jiang Wei said, "Are you mine, or are you for public use?"

All Siao Yu could do was harden her heart and bear the stench, dirt and disorder. You don't live here, anyway, Jiang Wei constantly said, his speech prickly with discontent. It was as if Siao Yu *wanted* to go live at the old man's house. Two weeks after their "wedding," the old man had come running over to say that the Immigration Department had stopped by early in the morning and asked him straight out where his "wife" had gone. He told them she had gone to work the morning shift. The next time if they came at night, he couldn't very well tell them she had gone to work the night shift, could he? The investigator from the Immigration Department had also seen several of Rita's dresses hanging up and had eyeballed the length of those dresses in comparison to Siao Yu's height in the wedding photos, then said, "If your wife is Chinese, how is it that she wears Italian dresses?"

Jiang Wei had no choice but to take Siao Yu the three blocks to the old man's house and to install her there. Even though the old man's house was dilapidated, there were two bedrooms, so she had her privacy. Siao Yu's room had only a half-bathroom, with no bath or shower, so she would have to pass through the old man's room in order to bathe. Jiang Wei very seriously checked the lock; it was in good working order and reliable. He told her, if the old creep tries to pull anything, just jump out the window and run over to my place. It's just three blocks away, and even if he chases after you, keep on running. Siao Yu laughed and replied, that won't happen. Jiang Wei asked on what basis she was so sure it wouldn't happen. Hearing such a young girl showering would even make a paralytic stand up!

"It won't happen. He has Rita." Siao Yu pointed to Rita, who was at this moment standing in the kitchen, scowling as she fried fish. Rita felt about Siao Yu just about the way Jiang Wei felt about the old man, and she took no pains to conceal it. After Siao Yu moved in, the old man no longer let Rita spend the night in his room. He said that if the Immigration Department were to come again, the whole story would be much too difficult to explain.

After she had lived away from the apartment for half a year, it fell into complete disarray. Siao Yu returned to the old man's place earlier and earlier all the time. Everything was cluttered at Jiang Wei's. Of the three guys, one had left and another had gotten himself a girl-friend who did piecework at home for a clothing factory, so every day she would sit in the apartment operating a sewing machine. The house had one more din and one less stench, but on balance it was about the same. No one spoke much to anyone else, but Siao Yu just could not study there. Every night after dinner, Jiang Wei would go to his night courses and Siao Yu would go to the old man's place. For whatever it was worth, she had her own room there, and if the old man and Rita weren't arguing or fighting, it was fairly quiet. She did-n't understand what it was they fought about. Money? The leaky roof? How to get rid of the cockroaches in the kitchen? How to keep the drains from clogging up? How the two of them were to eke out a living, each pressing the other to go out to put food on the table? Now approaching fifty, Rita never had a regular job. At the moment she depended on extravagant people ordering home-cooked

Italian food and pastries. Whether she earned a lot or a little depended on how many people had the whim of having an Italian feast catered in their homes.

After a while Siao Yu became aware that one of the things they argued about was her. Every evening, when Siao Yu came into the front yard, she groped in the dark to climb the front steps. But one evening, the porch light suddenly turned on. As she entered, she saw the old man standing in the doorway; obviously he had heard her footsteps and come running to turn on the light for her. Was he afraid she would stumble and fall? Was he worried that she was afraid of the dark? Was he afraid she would despise him for being too cheap even to turn on the porch light? She didn't make much noise when she walked, so he must have pinned down the exact time she would return and waited quietly so he could turn on the porch light for her. Was it possible that he was waiting for her? Why would he be waiting for her; hadn't he been playing cards with Rita? Not long after she entered her room, she heard a "moo!" sound—Rita making a noise just like a female beast. Then there was arguing, arguing, arguing; for arguing, Italian was the most passionately unrestrained and expressive of languages. The next morning, the old man sat crouching at the table trying to piece together their "wedding picture," the glass in the frame shattered beyond repair. She didn't dare to ask what was the matter. What need was there to ask? Slowly she picked up the glass shards off the floor as if it were her fault.

"Did Rita get angry?" she asked. The old man's eyes peered under his brow and over the top of his reading glasses—such effort. Yet she couldn't ask, why did you turn on the porch light for me? Out of protectiveness? Concern? Ingratiation? This matter was already awkward enough. If she were to seek answers, she would only end up embarrassing everyone.

The old man shrugged his shoulders as if to say, is there anything in the world more normal than getting angry? She stood stiffly for a while, then said, "Shouldn't you ask Rita to come back?" It wasn't all that difficult to muddle through the Immigration Department's investigation; they wouldn't burst in on them but would first use the doorbell and sound a warning. Once the doorbell rang, everybody could start acting. The house was a mess, so any pile of rubbish would serve to hide Rita. No, no, no. The more the old man said no, the more insistent he became. Siao Yu lowered her voice and put an envelope on the table. "Here are two weeks' rent."

The old man didn't look at it.

When she had walked over to the doorway, she turned around and saw he had dug the paper money out of the envelope and was in the process of counting it. His head was stretched forward as if he were eating something flaky and wanted to keep it over his plate. She knew he was anxious to count the money in order to determine whether it was the amount he expected. The last time he had raised the rent, Jiang Wei had come running over to haggle with him, and she was afraid they were going to end up killing each other. But this time the old man's neck had returned to its original position, as if he had eaten his fill, and she saw him smile to himself. Siao Yu wanted to mediate, so she paid the rent the old man had requested, with no intention of telling Jiang Wei. It was only ten dollars! Just give the old man this one petty pleasure.

After a fight, if Rita had stormed off, she would come back the next day, and the ensuing two or three days would be especially happy and harmonious. The old man would play the violin and she would sing. They would play and sing and get carried away: the table overflowed with plates and glasses, the floor was littered with playing cards and wine bottles, and the garbage can smelled like the plague. Siao Yu, hearing them from her room, was moved. She thought, they are constantly at each other's throats, yet in their violin playing and singing, they are so loving. They should get married, because other than the two of them appreciating each other, the rest of the world goes on as if they didn't exist. They should live together, neither rejecting the other, and even if they fought like animals, they could still lick each others' wounds.

She heard that before the old man had "married" her, he had

agreed to marry Rita. They had already been together for many years. But because she had been put in between them, they were denied even this rudimentary happiness.

Siao Yu's shame engulfed her. Quietly she tiptoed out to the kitchen to take out the garbage bag. She always did this sort of thing on the sly; otherwise Rita might feel she was violating her prerogatives, vying with her for the status of lady of the house. After she had cleared out the kitchen and washed her hands, she went out to the living room and saw the two of them standing face-to-face at the window. The violin bow had stopped, but the room still held a quivering final note that would not dissipate. Their song sang of two people destined to depend on each other, and at this moment they seemed as if they had fallen asleep peacefully while standing. Siao Yu was deeply, deeply moved.

It was the old man who first saw Siao Yu. He pushed Rita away, while she was in the act of kissing him, and grew flustered at the sight of this young woman who seemed to have walked into the scene by mistake. He picked up his violin and bow again, if only to conceal his awkwardness and embarrassment. He didn't play, however, but promptly dropped both arms down to his sides. Siao Yu wondered what was the matter with him. Was the expression on his face self-deprecation or shame? Perhaps in front of her—this young woman, this real living being—he despised himself and Rita and their hollowed-out existence. Their present state was not at all brought on by aging but definitely had to do with degeneration. By "marrying" him, Siao Yu suffered a loss of decency; her very association with him could itself be called a form of degeneracy. But her indecency was exceptional and conscious; his was compulsive and unconscious. How do you rectify something that is unconscious? Siao Yu had enough lifetime ahead of her to rectify a temporary bout of what people consider degenerate, but he did not have much time left. He had pushed Rita away, perhaps afraid that their vulgar pleasures would scare Siao Yu. It was as if Siao Yu, standing there so fresh, so young and unspoiled made him conscious that such pleasures were only fitting for a young woman like her with true life and youth.

All of this took place within an instant. Could an instant contain so much feeling? You can't be at all certain if the feeling you grasp in an instant is reality or illusion. This instant of time presented nothing unusual for Rita. She invited Siao Yu to join the festivities and encouraged the old man to play a song Siao Yu knew, while Rita poured her a large glass of wine.

"It's late. I have to get some sleep," she declined. "I have to work tomorrow."

She returned to her room, and after a while she heard the old man see Rita off. When she went to the bathroom to brush her teeth, she saw the old man sitting alone in the kitchen drinking wine, his two eyes empty. "Good night," he said without even looking at Siao Yu.

"Good night," she replied. "You should get to sleep. It's not good to drink too much." She always used this tone when speaking with disobedient patients.

"My back hurts. I think I probably slept *too* much."

Siao Yu hesitated a moment but finally walked over to him. He was bare-chested, his bones clearly defined, his belly still hanging down, baggy. His dyed hair had grown out, and he looked like a speckled hen. His two forearms were like hairy crab legs. Siao Yu sized him up while she gave him a back rub. When he said thank you, she stopped. Again he said good night, then stood up. She was just about to answer when he grasped her hand. She nearly cried out but controlled herself, because neither his bearing nor his expression revealed any ill intent. "You keep this place so clean. You always make *everything* so clean. Why? There are only three months left; aren't you just going to move out after that?"

"But you're going to go on living here," Siao Yu said.

"You still grow flowers in the front yard. When I die, the flowers will go on living. Was that what you were thinking?"

Siao Yu smiled noncommittally. She had never thought of it that way. Whatever she felt like doing, she just did it. Slowly, the old man smiled. What kind of a smile? A smile of a man rescued from crisis? Like a withered tree that blooms to life? With one hand he clasped

Siao Yu's hand and with the other he grasped his wine glass. After quietly drinking a mouthful, he asked, "What's your father like? Does he drink?"

"No!" she shook her head vigorously, and like a child refusing something, resolutely gathered her whole body in opposition.

The old man let out a sonorous "ha ha!" and kissed her on the forehead.

As she lay in bed, Siao Yu's heart was still beating fast. What had gotten into the old man? Should she report this to Jiang Wei? Before taking her away, would Jiang Wei punch the old man in the nose? "Trying to take advantage, you old beast?" he would curse him. But could you call that "taking advantage"? In her mind she reviewed the scene she had just experienced in all its minor details. It seemed the old man had become a different person. There was none of the tepid shamelessness she had become used to. Even though he was bare-chested and filthy, there was no trace of filth in his manner. He had asked her, does your father drink? He had not asked her what her boyfriend was like. He only compared himself to her father, not to her boyfriend. Maybe something had made him feel paternal toward her. His kiss had also been a paternal kiss.

On the weekend, she did not bring this up with Jiang Wei. Jiang Wei had bought an old car so he could drive to a better-paying job as a road maintenance worker. At this point, they could only do their business as a couple in that car. "Next month we'll be able to pay back all the money," he said with his brow knit. His skin was tanned dark, like a peasant's, and had not a single downy body hair on it. Siao Yu held him tightly, canceling out a load of disturbing recollections. She kissed him forcefully.

October is spring in Sydney. As Siao Yu was walking, a car rumbling like a tractor stopped alongside her. It was the old man's car.

"Why aren't you taking the train?" he asked her after she got into the car.

She replied that she had been walking to and from work for months now to save train fare. Suddenly the old man was silent. He had raised the rent three times and had the roof repaired, the plumbing unblocked and the cockroaches exterminated, charging Siao Yu half the expenses every time. Each time she had received a bill, she had immediately paid it without complaint, never breathing a word to Jiang Wei. If he found out, he'd argue and yell, accusing the old man while staring straight at Siao Yu. She would rather use her money to buy peace of mind. And if she hid the resulting hardships, no one would bother her. What else could she do? Jiang Wei wouldn't say, I'll quit smoking, I'll stop going to nightclubs, I'll skip eating out with my mates, and you use the money I save to take the train. He wouldn't do this; he could only raise a ruckus, and whether he won or lost the argument was secondary.

The old man finally spoke once they had gotten home. "No wonder you've gotten so thin." He had been thinking about this the whole way back. She thought he might say, next month when you pay the rent, keep back enough money to buy yourself a transit pass. But he didn't say it. The old man's flesh and bones, so thoroughly permeated with poverty, didn't contain this kind of generosity. At most, when he bought a used sofa, he refrained from presenting Siao Yu with a bill. Instead, Rita paid for half the sofa, and thereafter she occupied that sofa constantly as she smoked cigarettes, read the newspaper, painted her fingernails and toenails, or just stared off into space.

One day she stared at Siao Yu as the latter walked past her on her way to the bathroom and suddenly arched an eyebrow and laughed. After Siao Yu showered, she would always wipe down the bathtub and sink. The bathroom mirror was always cloudy and flecked with toothpaste. The sink always had a few hairs on it from the old man clipping his nose hairs. The colorful fingernail clippings on the floor were Rita's. The one part Siao Yu could never figure out were the dirty fingerprints on the soap; every day she would wash it, and every day they would reappear. When she was about to put her clothes on, she heard someone knocking at the bathroom door. In one spot where the white paint had peeled off the glass pane in the door, she saw an eye peeping at her, clashing strongly with the white-washed glass surrounding it. Siao Yu screamed at the top of her lungs, a blood-curdling screech. That eye was big enough to swallow you. Flustered, she pulled on her underclothes, and the person outside started to chortle. As she calmed down, she realized it was Rita's laugh. "Open the door, I've got to use the toilet right away!"

Rita hiked up her skirt, sat on the toilet and urinated with exuberance, making a sound like a driving rain. Once relieved, she heaved a sigh and shivered a few times while she used her large dark eyes to bite down on Siao Yu, masticating and tasting her half-naked body. "I just wanted to see if your boobs and bum were real!" she snickered.

Siao Yu didn't know how to take this comment from a woman who didn't even wear panties. Seeing her frantically putting the rest of her clothes on, Rita said, "Don't worry, he's not home." Lately, the old man had been going out every day, and not even Rita knew what he was up to.

"I'm telling you, I'm going to leave. I want to marry a decent man with money," Rita said. She held her head up high as she sat on the toilet. Siao Yu asked, what about the old man?

"Him? He's married to you, isn't he?" She smiled a wicked smile.

"That's not real, you know that!" Siao Yu blushed in shame.

"Aw, who the hell knows what's real and what's not?" Rita leaned back on the toilet seat, crossed her legs and lit a cigarette. After a while, she flicked a layer of ash onto the floor. "He behaves toward me like beast to beast, but toward you, it's like human to human."

"I'll be moving out soon!" Siao Yu said. "In fact, I can move out tomorrow."

Once again Siao Yu thought about how she'd been inserted into the middle of this and how it was making everything turn out badly. "Rita, don't go! You two should get married and spend your lives together!"

"Get married? That's for *people*. Beasts don't marry each other. There's no need! They just breed together, that's all! I've got to find the kind of man that, when you're together with him, you don't feel like some she-beast. It's strange: being with a human, a beast starts to be like a human; being with a beast, a human becomes like a beast!"

"But, Rita, he needs someone to take care of him. He's old now. . ."

"That's right, he's old! Two months from now the law allows you two to separate, and after another year it will allow you to divorce. What's left for *me*? He says when he dies, if just one person goes to his funeral, he won't have any regrets. Am I supposed to be that one person at his funeral?"

"He's still healthy. Why this talk about dying?"

"He drinks every day. He could die any day!"

"But he needs you, he loves you . . ."

"Aw, fuck him!"

Rita never came back. The old man drank very tranquilly. Siao Yu took this tranquility for heartsickness. While cleaning the bathroom, Siao Yu threw one of Rita's empty face powder compacts into the wastebasket, but quickly she found it restored to its original place. Siao Yu took this for nostalgia. The old man never mentioned Rita, yet more than once when the kettle was on, he would inadvertently call out, "Rita, the water's boiling." He no longer played the violin at home but did as Rita had always hoped he would: he went out to earn money. Siao Yu unexpectedly discovered why the old man went out every day: he was selling his art.

It was a weekend, and Jiang Wei drove Siao Yu to the seashore to see a handicraft fair. Someone there was playing the violin. The sea wind was strong, and the melody blew past, a measure here and a measure there, but Siao Yu could tell it was the sound of the old man's violin. They walked through half the marketplace and still did not see the violinist, just heard the tune intermittently weaving its way through the crowd. It was only when the wind came up strongly and an inexplicable rain sent people scattering for shelter, emptying the whole street, that the old man suddenly appeared.

Siao Yu had been pulled by Jiang Wei under the large parasol of an ice cream stand. "Hey, it's him!" Jiang Wei pointed toward the old man with surprise. "Fiddling for food! Not bad—at least he's eating off his own labor!"

The old man was also busy trying to find someplace to get out of the rain. Siao Yu called to him, but he didn't hear her. Jiang Wei scolded her: "What are you calling him for? I don't know that guy."

In his haste, the old man dropped his hat. While he was retrieving it, the buckles on his violin case popped open and the violin fell out. He picked up the violin with both hands and checked it all over, as if checking an infant to see where it might be hurt. An errant wind curled some of the old man's paper money out of the violin case and sent it scurrying. Only this pulled the old man's attention away from his violin and in an instant sent him on a panicked chase.

Gradually it rained harder. In the empty street only the old man was left, doing a dance with his hands and feet as if catching bees and butterflies, capturing the paper money on the wind.

As soon as Siao Yu made a move, she was restrained. "Stay put!" Jiang Wei said. "Don't embarrass me. People will wonder if you have something to do with that old tramp." Still, she struggled to release herself from him. Bill by bill, she chased down the old man's hard day's earnings. When the old man saw her and recognized her, he was drenched from head to foot. As he stepped forward on the slick pavement, he slipped and fell. She walked over to help, clutching a handful of bills. Half squatting and half kneeling there, he looked up at her with gratitude, as if the earnings she'd gathered were not being returned to him but bestowed on him. As she helped him to his feet, she looked over to find Jiang Wei and saw a vacant space where he'd been standing.

Jiang Wei's room was also vacant. Siao Yu waited for him for two hours, but he did not return. She knew how touchy he could be about such things. One day after Rita had gone, the old man came back with a hanging orchid abandoned by someone who had moved. Siao Yu had stacked up two stools and climbed atop them to hang the orchid while the old man had held her ankles tightly. Jiang Wei just happened to arrive at that moment, and the door just happened to be unlocked. The old man told him, come on in and pour yourself a glass of water, we're in the middle of something.

"We? How dare he refer to you and him as 'we'? So you two have become 'we'?" Jiang Wei had said in the car with a look of disgust. "Two people water flowers together, cut the grass together, maybe sit in a room together and watch a little TV or read a book. No wonder he's talking 'we'." Siao Yu was shocked: it turned out he had been keeping her and the old man under surveillance! "From what I can see, it looks like the old husband and the young wife are having a pretty good life together!"

"What is this nonsense you're talking?!" This was the first time Siao Yu had used an explosive tone like this when addressing Jiang Wei. But she immediately softened her tone again: "You know how people, when they spend time together, often end up having friendly relations . . ."

"Even with an old bastard, an old good-for-nothing like that, you can still live on with him, having 'friendly relations'?" He intentionally used the words most prone to ambiguity.

"Jiang Wei!" she yelled. She wanted to yell: you're being so unfair! But tumultuous sobbing blocked her throat. The parked car shuddered from her suppressed sobs, and soon she forced herself to calm down. She feared if she cried, Jiang Wei's heart would be even more desperate. That mood of his would pass as long as he could indulge himself sexually in her complete tenderness. No mood ever prevented him from wanting her, not even suffering or rage. "What kind of a girl are you, anyway?" he would ask spasmodically while on top of her.

Siao Yu paced the floor of the apartment waiting for Jiang Wei. When he said something outrageous, she would never respond in kind. If a man says such terrible things, he must be even more terribly wounded. She waited straight through until midnight, but she waited in vain. When she returned to the old man's place, he was half-reclining on the living room sofa, his facial color very bad. He smiled at her.

She also smiled at him. There was a strange sort of meeting between their two smiles.

The next day when she returned from work, she saw him lying in the exact same position, smiling toward her in exactly the same way. Both of them smiled at each other again. In the kitchen, she discovered that all the plates, bowls, pots and pans were in the exact same places as before. The old man had not used them or even touched them. What's the matter with him? She shot out to ask him, but he just smiled again. Only a person who felt completely at ease could smile such a smile. She convinced herself to suppress this strange feeling coming from nowhere. She started to clean the house so that when she moved out, she would leave the old man a fresher, more humane abode. She hoped that anything that passed through her hands would become better: nothing in this world was of necessity destined for ruin, including even this old man who had already ruined half his life.

The old man saw Siao Yu busy at work. He knew this was her last day here, and the next day the two of them would go their separate ways. She would leave behind her an old, run-down but pleasant dwelling and an isolated and lonely but untroubled old man.

The old man had changed. What had caused him to change, Siao Yu couldn't quite comprehend. Her impression of the old man was that he was always looking for lost things: shoehorns, reading glasses, razor blades. Once a chair broke, and under the cushion he found a tiny image of a saint that he had been searching for for nearly forty years. His joy was so mysterious and mystical that even Rita couldn't fathom what story was contained in the thumbnail-sized image. Finding this image was as if, by chance, he had found a part of himself that had been long lost. The part of him that was tranquil and refined.

Nowadays he would take out a trash bag that wasn't yet full, and when he came in he would look at Siao Yu as if to say: see, I'm doing chores, I'm living a proper life. And he really was living properly: he no longer approached the neighbor's doorstep to read their newspaper, and he never again extorted payment from the occasional car that wanted to park on the edge of his yard. He still liked to go around the house shirtless, but whenever Siao Yu returned, he would immediately put on a shirt. He still liked to watch TV with the volume turned up loud enough to wake the dead, but as soon as the light went out in Siao Yu's room, he would immediately twist the dial down to the point where it was almost inaudible. One day when Siao

Yu was on her way to work, she saw the old man carrying his violin in the peaceful morning sunlight. Self-reliance had lent the old man a healthy and conscientious expression and a dignified demeanor. She was deeply moved. He was such a proper old man, the kind of old man who had proper feelings toward the world and his fellow human beings.

While Siao Yu was in the yard raking leaves she thought, he can live on well, even without Rita and without me. She looked into the window and saw the old man stirring, trying with all his might to move. He seemed to be trying to use his arms to propel his whole body forward but soon failed. He tried again and again, each time more fiercely than the last, but finally he gave up, reclining back to his original position.

So it's because he can't move! Siao Yu rushed back into the living room. He saw her and gave that same smile again. So he would have kept smiling like that until she left, letting her leave on time with a peaceful heart . . . ? She called the emergency number. A doctor and a nurse came and confirmed what Siao Yu had suspected. That fall he had taken in the rain had had consequences: the old man had suffered a stroke. They also told her that the old man's condition was very bad: at best he might still be alive after a week, and if he were, he could live on, immobile, but not for more than a few more days. They did not take the old man back with them to the hospital in the ambulance.

The old man was now lying in his own bed, surrounded by racks of bottles with rubber tubes. Every six hours a nurse would come by to check on him, feed him something and change the bottles. "What is your relationship to him?" the nurse asked. Compared with this wretched old patient, the nurse seemed like a snooty socialite.

The old man was still helpless and unable to speak. The telephone rang, and Siao Yu took to her heels, grateful for this reprieve.

"Have you packed your things yet?" Jiang Wei was calling from a very noisy place. When he heard that she had not yet packed, he became angry. "You've got two hours. Pack your things and wait for me outside the door. I don't want to see that guy!" It sounds like he doesn't want to see me either, Siao Yu thought. Ever since that rainy day when she had brought the old man back to his house, Jiang Wei had avoided her. She had gone to their apartment to wait for him a few times, but she had never seen him. When she asked him on the telephone if he was very busy, he would answer the question not asked: goddammit, I've had enough! He behaved as though he were the only one who had made a sacrifice this year, as though only he suffered from all this underhanded business, only he were making all the concessions. "Don't forget," Jiang Wei emphasized against the noisy background. "Ask him for those three days' rent back. You're moving out three days before the end of the month!"

"He's taken very ill. It might be dangerous . . ."

"What's *that* got to do with the rent?"

She repeated that he could die at any moment. He said, what's that got to do with *you?*

Yes, that's right. What's that got to do with me? Thinking of this, she went to her room, grabbing clothes left and right to pack. Suddenly she put them down and walked into the old man's room.

The nurse had left. The old man appeared to have fallen asleep. Just when she thought of leaving, he opened his eyes. This was it: this time they *had* to say goodbye. Her heart could not find a single word.

"I thought you'd gone already," the old man spoke first. She shook her head. What did she mean by shaking her head? That she wasn't leaving? She certainly hadn't said that she wanted to stay, and yet Jiang Wei had asked: how long do you plan to stay there, keep him company, take care of him in his old age, bury him . . . ?

From somewhere the old man pulled out and fingered a small card: it was a monthly train pass. He gestured to Siao Yu to take it. She did, and his face bore the calm expression of one who had confessed his sins.

"The nurse asked me who you were. I told her you were my tenant, that you were a really, really good kid," the old man said.

Siao Yu shook her head again. She really didn't know whether she was good. Just now on the telephone, Jiang Wei had been gnashing his teeth, saying that if she could get along so well living with an old good-for-nothing like that, she couldn't possibly be a "good" woman. He also told her that after two hours, he would drive past the house. If she wasn't standing in the doorway, he would turn the car around and leave. After that, he would not trouble her any further; she could keep the old man company as long as she liked. Once more he said that he had had enough.

The old man's eyes saw her off to the door. She turned back to say goodbye and saw the old man's slippers, one with its sole facing skyward. When she stooped to rearrange it, she suddenly realized that the old man might never have use for shoes again; her considerate gesture toward the old man was merely a sharp reminder of this. A reminder of what it meant to her? It was an excuse. She needed an excuse to stay with him a while longer, to do something more for him.

"I'll come back to see you . . ."

"Don't come back . . ." His eyes looked out the window as if to say, it's so nice out there, why come back in once you're out? The old man's hands moved. Siao Yu felt her own hands had the urge to move as well. Her hands clasped the old man's in hers.

"If . . ." the old man looked at her, his mouth full of things to say, yet he didn't speak. His eyes became bigger, apparently startled by his own temerity. She didn't ask what "if" was meant to ask. If you were to stay a few days, wouldn't it be wonderful? If I die, will you remember me? If I'm fortunate enough to have a funeral, will you attend it? If in the future you see a friendless old man, will you think of me?

Siao Yu nodded her head and affirmed his "if."

The old man's head slid down, and the tears collecting in his cavernous eye sockets were finally released.

Notes to "Siao Yu"

Page 157 **Siao Yu:** pronounced "shyao yh" and usually written Xiao Yu. We have used the spelling Siao Yu to provide easy cross-identification with the movie based on this story that uses this title and spelling. Xiao means "little" or "small," and the "yh" character is that for "fishing village."

Page 161 **Foreigner:** Chinese words for foreigners (*waiguoren*, meaning "outside country person" or, as here, *lao wai*) are generally used by Chinese in an absolute sense to designate non-Chinese, regardless of location.

Page 162 **"such a pig":** literally *Zhu Bajie*, the name of an anthropomorphic pig-man character in the picaresque classic *Journey to the West*.

Page 162 **Zhong Kui, Fan Li, Xi Shi:** arias from Chinese opera based on classical stories. Zhong Kui was a fearsome-looking but benevolent and lonely deity who was reluctant to part with his little sister but wanted her to have a happy married life. Xi Shi and Fan Li were lovers during the Warring States Period who, for the sake of their country Yue, agreed that Xi Shi be sent as a concubine to the King of Wu to use her beauty and feminine wiles to distract him into abandoning his plans to conquer Yue.

Geling Yan Born in Shanghai, Geling Yan was inducted into the People's Liberation Army at the age of twelve and served in both ballet and folk dance troupes. She began writing in the late 1970's as a correspondent covering the Sino-Vietnamese border war. Upon receiving her discharge from the Army, Yan moved to Beijing and published her first novel, *Green Blood*. Yan has published prolifically in the People's Republic of China, Taiwan and Hong Kong, where she has won a number of prestigious literary awards. Her work includes *Female Grasslands, Fusang* (currently being translated into English) and four other novels, as well as three short story collections and several screenplays, including the screenplay for *Xiu Xiu, The Sent Down Girl* (adapted from her short story "Celestial Bath"). *White Snake and Other Stories* is the first of her works to be published in English. Yan currently resides in the San Francisco Bay Area.

Lawrence A. Walker Born in Palo Alto, California, Walker is fluent in Chinese, Spanish, German, French and Portuguese. He received his B.S. in Languages and Linguistics from Georgetown University and his M.B.A. from University of Illinois at Champaign-Urbana. After serving a little over a decade as a Foreign Service Officer (including tours of duty in China, Germany and Mexico), he returned to the United States to work as the Managing Director of the German-American Chamber of Commerce in San Francisco. He now lives in the San Francisco Bay Area with his wife, Geling Yan Walker.

aunt lute books is a multicultural women's press that has been committed to publishing high quality, culturally diverse literature since 1982. In 1990, the Aunt Lute Foundation was formed as a non-profit corporation to publish and distribute books that reflect the complex truths of women's lives and the possibilities for personal and social change. We seek work that explores the specificities of the very different histories from which we come, and that examines the intersections between the borders we all inhabit.

Please write, phone or e-mail (books@auntlute.com) us if you would like us to send you a free catalog of our other books or if you wish to be on our mailing list for future titles. You may buy books directly from us by phoning in a credit card order or mailing a check with the catalog order form.

Please visit our website at www.auntlute.com.

Aunt Lute Books
P.O.Box 410687
San Francisco, CA 94141
(415)826-1300

This book would not have been possible without the kind contributions of the Aunt Lute Founding Friends:

Anonymous Donor
Anonymous Donor
Rusty Barcelo
Marian Bremer
Diane Goldstein

Diana Harris
Phoebe Robins Hunter
Diane Mosbacher, M.D., Ph.D.
William Preston, Jr.
Elise Rymer Turner